Two Trees Hollow

Sweetspring is a quiet western town until an itinerant gang of robbers causes havoc. Wesley Vernon, a twenty-four-year-old mine engineer, thinks he recognizes the robbers' leader as a childhood friend and determines to bring him to justice. Before he sets off he is devastated to learn that his intended bride, Maddy, has been promised to a wealthy banker from Boston.

Never could Wes have imagined how his moral courage would be tested as he faces gun battles, bank raids, a prison breakout and coming face-to-face with his childhood friend, and then, incredibly, with Maddy's suitor. Further complications ensue with a chance meeting with Alice, a devious beauty, who plays a dangerous game of her own.

Two Trees Hollow

Frank Chandler

A Black Horse Western

ROBERT HALE

© Frank Chandler 2018
First published in Great Britain 2018

ISBN 978-0-7198-2768-6

The Crowood Press
The Stable Block
Crowood Lane
Ramsbury
Marlborough
Wiltshire SN8 2HR

www.bhwesterns.com

Robert Hale is an imprint
of The Crowood Press

1

It was about an hour after midday and the fortnightly wages wagon was due. There was a buzz of anticipation in the yard. The men had started to emerge from the mineshafts. They were beginning to gather in small groups, chatting loudly, bragging about their intended exploits with a pocketful of cash, or regaling their friends with tales of half-remembered shenanigans after the last payday. Tonight Sweetspring would be painted red in every possible shade and hue, until at least half the money had filled the coffers of the town's many drinking holes or lined the heavy-duty cash boxes in the several bordellos. Dancing would last well into the early hours of the morning, fights would break out all over town, but rarely was much damage done; gunshots were never heard as the sheriff enforced a strict no side-arms rule on payday.

Sitting in the dust or leaning against the stacks of pine pit props, tired and hot from their hours underground, this was the day everyone looked forward to. Everyone except the miners' wives. For too many of those ill-used women, in their own weak way, with threats of no meals, no clean clothes or the withdrawal of conjugal duties, would ambush their men-folk for some housekeeping money. Whatever they managed to get would disappear within a day or two clearing the slate with the dry goods merchant, or the doctor, the butcher, the baker and the candlestick maker. What was left, if anything, soon ran out and the town's tradesmen began to chalk up the next fortnight's credit before a day had passed. The only good thing about the endless circle for the men was the wages wagon and the fun that followed. Otherwise it was a bleak and hard life. And what a life – it was just like the dreary mineshafts, on and on into the dark of the unknown until the silver ran out. Then a new shaft and another, and then one day there would be nothing, the lodes all worked out. What then?

Wesley Vernon, one of the young mine foremen, walked across the yard towards the office and up the outside wooden stairs two at a time. He pushed open the door. The mine owner, Tor Gudrun, a second generation Swede, was sitting behind his desk shuffling some papers.

'Wages wagon's due,' Wes observed.

Tor looked up from the papers; he was lost in his own thoughts. 'These latest surveys aren't good. We'll have to cut some new shafts soon and hope we find another rich vein or . . .'

'Or?'

'Or I don't know what. Listen, Wes, I'd like you and your team to have another look further down the shaft we closed two months ago. Blow another side tunnel. What do you think? Can you do that?'

Wes laughed, 'Of course I can do it. There's no one better than me for blowing away the mountains!'

'Good, see to it as soon as you can. Now, look . . .'

But whatever Gudrun was about to say, he didn't finish. Two gunshots rang out. Wes ran to the window. Four masked horsemen had entered the yard and the two armed guards on the gate lay motionless in the dirt. The mineworkers were fixed to their places; nobody dared move. Three of the horsemen circled the yard, guns drawn, signalling a clear intention to bring down anyone who wanted to resist. There would be no resistance, of course, as the workmen were forbidden to carry guns on the premises. The fourth gunman had leapt down and was already at the door to the office. Wes had made a quick play for the gun rack on the office wall, but his hand was no more than loosely round the barrel of a Winchester when the door was kicked open.

'No, no, don't do that! Let go and put those hands up high.'

Tor Gudrun and Wes Vernon had no choice but to comply. The masked man put his gun to Gudrun's head and pushed him and Wes out through the door.

'Stay calm, everyone, or this man's brains will see the light of day.'

It was perfectly obvious what was going on. The riders had clearly been staking out, waiting for a sighting of the money wagon. Once they'd seen it in the valley, they made their move and, sure enough, the sound of the horses was getting louder. One of the horsemen had removed the dead guards from the gateway and, standing there casually as the wagon came into the yard, he fired just once, killing the shotgun. The driver pulled up and, seeing the situation, raised his hands in the air. Pushing Gudrun and Wes down the steps, the gang leader had everything under control. The wagon driver was forced to turn the wagon round and head out of the yard. Two of the riders followed the wagon. The fourth rider brought the leader's horse over, he mounted up and they both rode out. The entire episode had taken no more than a few minutes, although time was quite irrelevant. For a moment, nobody moved. It was an eerie moment of almost total silence apart from the staccato of the office door banging in the wind. There was a stunned inertia apart from the two large tumbleweeds blowing in through the gate. The yard was in shocked silence before conversation suddenly burst out. There were shouts of 'get after them,' 'kill the bastards,' 'that's our money,' and the like. Gudrun held up his hands to calm the angry workforce.

'Won't do no good following them. Let's just hope they let the driver go. They'll just take the cash box and we've no hope of catching them.'

Word soon spread and more miners came up out of the shafts to see what was going on. One of the gang foremen came over to the office.

'What the heck?'

'Robbing sonsofbitches,' Gudrun said. 'They won't get away with this.'

'Too late,' Wes said plainly.

'But why do it here in the yard?' Tor Gudrun slapped his hand down on the stair rail. 'We'll have to put more men on the wagon next time, more guards on the gate, more expense, always more expense just when we're up against the wall. We ain't never had anything like this. This is a peaceful place.'

'Not any more,' observed Wes. 'That's why they robbed us under our noses here in the yard. Next, they'll want protection money.'

Tor Gudrun threw his hands in the air. 'They've got away with a huge haul and our next funds from the smelters don't come in for a week. It's a bad day for the mine. One more raid like that and I'll be bankrupt.'

Wes had no idea the mine was in financial trouble; silver ore was still coming out of the ground. True, there was less of it, but he'd open another hole and they'd find a crossvein somewhere. Deep in thought, he scuffed the dirt with the toe of his boot.

Gudrun could see Wes was thinking. 'What's on your mind?'

'Nothin' really. Just got a hunch.'

'About?'

'Dunno,' Wes replied vaguely. He looked up into the sky, chewing his tongue. 'Somethin's botherin' me. Not rightly sure what.'

Slowly, the yard returned to normal, except that there was no money to distribute for the men's wages and there were three bodies to take back to town for burial. Gudrun sent the men home; there'd be no more productivity after the robbery. He told them he would get a loan from the bank to cover the wages. Another cashbox would be delivered, but for tonight and this weekend the men would have to hope the saloon owners would be willing to chalk up credit, and the wives would just have keep quiet until Monday. It was a tall order.

'Let's go and talk about the new shaft you're going to blow.' Gudrun turned away and went back up to his office. Wes followed. They stood in front of the mine-shaft map.

Unlike most of the miners, Wes didn't live from hand to mouth. He wasn't a miser, but he wanted a better life and for that he knew he should save some of his wages. Consequently, instead of needing credit, he had some spare cash to spend on his girl at the dance that night.

Maddy was a lovely girl, the daughter of a wealthy entrepreneur, Harry Mancini. She was one of those girls that any man would be proud to take on his arm, of a good height and slim, with shining shoulder-length chestnut hair and alluring green eyes. She was still very shy and totally unaware of her appeal. Two years ago her father sent her back east to a smart college. During the holidays she lodged with relatives in a Boston suburb. Coming back to the far west had been a bit of a shock for Maddy to say the least of it. Used to sophisti-cated people, pretentious parties and cultured society, the West now seemed grubby and squalid. She couldn't understand why her father wanted to live out west when true American society lived almost exclusively in the east. The business opportunities in the west for fast money was something a young girl bedazzled by eastern society wouldn't understand.

Harry Mancini didn't like the west any more than his wife or daughter did; however, the chances to become unbelievably rich were very favourable for a smart entrepreneur. His fingers were in every conceivable pie from beef to silver, from flour to guns. But there were risks too. One risk that was completely unforeseen was that his daughter Maddy would fall hopelessly in love with a totally unsuitable young mine foreman with very limited prospects. This wasn't why Harry Mancini had laid out a small fortune in her east coast education. He had his eyes on becoming state governor and the right kind of marriage for his daughter was part of that plan. The young man who threatened this was Wes Vernon.

Mancini had been the town mayor, chairman of the local cattle association, an important financier of two local silver mines, head of the town council, and a much-respected local businessman. He now had his eye on the office of state governor, but first he had to secure a major political role. The next state elections were due soon and Mancini hoped to get a position in the office of Governor Bradley if he was re-elected. Mancini could count on very significant support: his wife Belle was a relative to Governor Washburn in Massachusetts and Mancini was hoping Maddy might form a relationship with the Laroche banking family in Boston. She met the very eligible son, Emile, while at college there. It was part of Mancini's plan; such an arrangement would increase his credentials, his influence and his financial backing immeasurably.

Judging by the rowdy noise and the high spirits in

11

Sweetspring that night, there had been no problem in the mineworkers getting credit. Nor were they the only men spending their hard-earned dollars, in cash or credit, on strong beer and women. The dance halls were full of the whole gamut of Sweetspring society: railroad survey teams, labourers, cattle ranchers, cowboys, drifters and, in the better establishments, the cream of Sweetspring society, the gentlemen and their ladies, like Harry and Belle Mancini.

Mothers can sometimes be less severe than fathers, a little more understanding and a little more devious. Belle Mancini no more approved of her daughter's young man than her husband did, but she had a better plan to deal with it. Every Friday she allowed Maddy to go to one of the less salubrious dance halls with the unsuitable Wes for just two hours, provided that she rejoined her parents with Wes later in the evening. What Belle mistakenly thought was that if she let Maddy spend time alone with Wes she would soon tire of his uncouth, uneducated company. They would be able to show up his lack of suitability and quietly but unkindly denigrate him. Of course, Maddy was not allowed to be entirely alone with Wes: one of the Mancini's many servants acted as chaperone to ensure Maddy's reputation was not tainted.

Wes and Maddy had been at Jake's Saloon for about an hour, dancing and chatting. Wes drained the remains of his beer, put down his glass and swung Maddy out of her seat. 'C'mon, let's dance the night away!'

Maddy loved it when Wes whirled her round the

12

dance floor. She loved dressing up for the dances. She loved having her hair combed by one of the maidservants ready for the Friday dance. She just loved being with Wes and couldn't understand why her parents were so against him. She smiled at him.

'Were you in any danger today? I mean it was a shocking thing to happen. When I heard about it, my first thought was for you.'

Wes shook his head. 'No, I wasn't in any danger, but it was a very frightening thing being robbed like that. Tor Gudrun had a gun held to his head, three men shot to death and no chance of defending ourselves. We should have been better prepared after the other robberies in the town last month and the reports of cattle rustling in the neighbourhood. We haven't had this kind of lawlessness here. . . .' He suddenly looked away, staring into the distance. Something had stirred a memory. He stopped dancing right in the middle of the dance floor.

'What is it, Wes?'

'It's just occurred to me.'

Maddy frowned. 'What has? We can't stand here like this. We'd better move to the side.'

They went back to their chairs and sat down, Wes was still distant, deep in thought. Then he slapped the table.

'That's it! I didn't realize why it was bothering me. Now I know. I'm sure, and I think I might be able to do something about it.'

'Wes, for goodness' sake, stop talking in riddles.'

'These aren't riddles,' he said, 'this might just be the solution.'

13

Maddy frowned, shaking her head in despair.

'Listen, we're going back to your parents. I know we could stay here for another hour, but this is mighty important and I need to talk to your pa.'

'Father,' Maddy corrected. 'Call him my father, not pa. Oh, Wes.'

But Wes wasn't listening to her; a greater urgency was overriding the niceties of language. He pushed the batwings aside; he almost dragged Maddy out of the saloon and the chaperone had a hard time keeping up with them.

'I think this will change your pa's mind about me!'

2

Walking back along a side street to her parents in the Grand Hotel, Maddy slowed down and tugged at Wesley's hand. The Grand Hotel, which was grander in name than it was in reality, was where the town's older society gathered in the saloon for what the young folk thought were boring conversations about family and business. They played genteel games of cards and were very restrained with their drinking. The dancing was to a smart band of somewhat variable musical skill, but a cut above the banjo and fiddle in Jake's saloon. Sweetspring was a growing sprawl on the edge of the long mountain range in Argent County, which occupied a barren part of southern Nevada. The community was mostly divided between tradesmen and workers on the one hand, and entrepreneurs and professional people on the other. The two halves rarely mixed, except when romantic attachment crossed the social boundaries, as it did for Wes and Maddy.

'What is it?' he asked.

Maddy looked down at her feet.

'C'mon,' he encouraged her. 'Tell me what's on your mind.' He took her up a couple of steps onto the boardwalk and sat her down on a bench.

'I wasn't going to say anything about it, but you've got to know. I don't want you to be talking to my parents without knowing what's just happened. Sometimes I think about what it will be like to be married, Wes. To have a home of my own, raise a family, look after my man . . .'

'We'll have all that one day, Mads. One day when I've saved enough money to persuade your folks I'm good enough.'

'They're parents, Wes, not folks. And that's just it, you're never going to be good enough for my father to agree.'

Wes frowned. 'He doesn't have to agree. Not if we truly want to be with each other. We can overcome all that "who's suitable" stuff.'

'I wish that were true.'

'Look, Mads,' he began, but Maddy put her hand gently over his mouth. 'No, listen to me. My father wants me to be engaged to a man who's coming here soon, someone he's calling a business partner. He says it will be a good match and this man comes from a very wealthy family in Boston.'

'Boston? Isn't that where you went to school? Did you know this man, then?'

'Not really, Wes, it's nothing like that. I did meet him but I want to marry you, not someone from Boston, just because he's rich.'

'How old is he?'

16

'I don't know, it doesn't matter. I'm not something to be traded like railroad bonds. The thing is my parents don't want me to see you any more.'

'What? When did all this blow up? Today, yesterday, when? And what do you know about railway bonds, for heaven's sake?'

Maddy put her arm round his shoulder and stroked his face with her hand. 'Sssh, quietly,' she said, 'or my chaperone will hear what we're talking about. You've got to pretend you don't know what I've just told you . . .'

'How can I pretend that? Your father is about to take away the only thing I care about and you want me to pretend.'

'You must or you'll lose me,' she said firmly, and stood up.

Wes got up too and they set off again.

'This changes everything, Maddy. I can't talk to your parents and pretend I don't know. I can't do that. You said you wanted to marry me. Do you still want to? Not now, I mean one day, when the time is right, would you wait?'

'If I could, I'd try.'

Wes didn't want to press the point any further. The conversation was at an end. Then, just as they were about to step off the boardwalk, there was a sudden commotion at the far end of the street. Four horsemen came tearing along towards Wes and Maddy, firing their pistols into the air, whooping and shouting. Wes pulled Maddy back into the shelter of the boardwalk. They ducked down as splinters showered. The shots weren't aimed at them; they were just four cowboys shooting randomly. The horsemen turned into Main Street. Wes got up and ran after them. This being dance night, he had no side-arm of any use, just a small boot pistol for close-up protection.

As he cornered the block he saw the riders pull up outside the Grand Hotel. They burst in through the main doors. Shots were fired and they emerged almost at once, mounted up and spurred out.

Several men ran out of the saloon but none had any useful weapon to hand.

A few revolver shots were fired from the riders. One of them shouted, 'A friendly warning!' before the night and the dust covered their departure.

Wes ran back to fetch Maddy.

'What was all that?' she asked nervously.

'I've no idea, but we'd better get to the hotel; they fired a few shots in there.'

'My parents!'

They hastened on in silence. Wes had forgotten temporarily what Maddy had just told him about a suitor from Boston. He was more worried about what they might find in the hotel saloon.

Mr and Mrs Mancini were fine. Nobody had been injured but the hotel saloon's ceiling and a couple of paintings had sustained a few holes. The big mirror behind the bar was now in shards on the floor, likewise a couple of windowpanes. The barkeep was already busy with a brush. Within moments the evening continued as if this was an everyday occurrence of no importance. On the first point it certainly wasn't an everyday event, but on the second point it would soon become clear to the Sweetspring community that this was far from a happening of no importance.

As the saloon returned to normal, the card games resumed, the band struck up a new dance number and conversation drowned out the sound of glass being swept up. Wes approached Mr and Mrs Mancini. He didn't want to prolong the meeting.

'Good evening, Mrs Mancini. Good evening, sir. I've things to attend to, so I've brought your daughter back early.' He was hoping to turn and go, but Mr Mancini caught his arm.

'Bad do this afternoon, Wesley. I understand you were involved in the robbery.'

'Not exactly involved, sir, just an onlooker.'

'But an unpleasant experience, nonetheless,' Mancini continued. 'I heard a gun was held to your head.'

'Not exactly, sir. The mine owner, Mr Gudrun, was held hostage for a moment. Fortunately they met no resistance from anyone, just took the wagon with the cash box and rode off, but they killed our two gate guards and the shotgun rider on the wagon, and the driver is still missing. Anyway, I'll bid you goodnight.'

This time he turned smartly and left, hoping his language had met with Maddy's approval. He hated having to think about the words he used and the way he talked, but he loved Maddy too deeply not to comply with her wishes and he desperately wanted to look fit enough to be the Mancinis' son-in-law. But with what Maddy had told him tonight, that seemed to be an unlikely dream.

Walking back down Main Street, so many things were whirling round in his mind. One of them he had wanted to share with Mr Mancini, as he was a man of considerable importance in the town. The news about a suitor from Boston had changed all that. But the riders in the town had made him think again about the robbery. Was it just a coincidence that there was a bunch of wild robbers at the mine, and now a bunch of wild cowboys shouting out a warning in the town? What could the 'friendly warning' be about? Only one thing kept nagging away at Wesley's subconscious, and the more he thought about it the more he was sure. He decided to pay the sheriff a visit tomorrow.

The following morning, Wes woke up with an appetite for bacon and beans. The frying pan was sitting on the stove and within minutes a good fire was heating things up. Wes cut himself some slices of fatty pork and put them in the pan. Unkindly, it spat back at him. He put some beans in a saucepan of cold water and the coffee pot to warm. The kettle would soon boil and he could add water to both. While the stove was doing its thing, he pushed open the door and went out onto the little covered veranda that adorned the front of his shack. Like most of the workmen at the mine, he lived in the spreading community of wooden huts just a couple of miles from the edge of Sweetspring. On his small fenced plot he grew a few vegetables and kept a pig. This was nothing unusual. The mine owner, Tor Gudrun, had been a pig farmer back in Sweden before immigrating to America, and he'd encouraged his workers to keep pigs for food. Not many of the workers could be bothered, except those that were married, and then the wife tended the house and the animals, as they should. Wes was more adventurous than most of the single men. He even grew carrots and sweetcorn in his bit of dirt.

He rolled a smoke and sat on the little rocking chair that he had made with a few sticks of wood and some ingenuity. The sun was rising and the front of his shack got the best of the early morning heat. He was pondering what to do with the information which was causing him some concern; information about the robbery at the mine, something which had been bothering him ever since he stood near the gang leader holding a gun to Gudrun's head. The only thing to do was to talk to the sheriff. Up to now, Wes hadn't had anything to do with Sheriff Cottrell and didn't know whether he was trustworthy or not. The information that Wes had could jeopardize his safety if given to the wrong person.

3

Clearing away his breakfast pans and swallowing the last mouthful of coffee, Wes buckled up his gun-belt and checked his six-gun; he examined the cylinder and spun it round to see each chamber was loaded. He saddled his horse and rode down slowly from the mine into Sweetspring. He was in no hurry; he kept running over the facts in his mind and thinking through how he was going to present them to the sheriff. Deep in thought, he hardly noticed the passing of two miles, at least not until he came to within a stone's throw of the town and could hear a deal of yelling and whooping – most unusual for early morning in Sweetspring. Then he heard the gunshots, random, plenty of them. He spurred his horse and got into Main Street as a bunch of horsemen were riding out of the other end. They were too distant to shoot at, and in any case Wes didn't know exactly what was going on.

Sheriff Sam Cottrell burst out of his office, still loading a Winchester. At the same time one of the bank tellers, Charlie Dobson, came out of the bank clutching his chest where a dark red patch was spreading. He looked dazed and sank to his knees. The bank manager, Herbert Grenfell, was next to come out, running to catch hold of Dobson before he toppled over.

'Hang in there, Charlie,' Grenfell said, then looking down the street saw the sheriff. 'Sam! Sam! Charlie needs a doctor.'

'And I need a posse!' Sam shouted back.

Wes quickly summed up the situation. There was no time to wait for the sheriff to get a posse together. The only hope of tracking the gang was to get after them without delay. He kicked the flanks of his horse as a swirl of dust caught him in the eye. Head down, he raced along Main Street.

The sheriff saw his intention. 'Hey, young man! Wait! Wait for a posse, it's too dangerous . . .'

But the words tailed off with the dust that blew down the street. Wes was already out of earshot. There was only one thing on his mind: to track the gang. Putting two and two together he surmised that the bank had been robbed and Charlie Dobson had been shot. He didn't know if the gang had got away with any cash or bonds or what: his sense of duty had kicked in without hesitation. It was clear the riders had been up to no good, whether the robbery had been successful or not. Either way it was another unwelcome disturbance to Sweetspring, which was a peaceful place except on dance night, but three more very bad incidents in the space of two days would put the whole community in fear of their lives.

Only the faint clouds of dust gave Wes any clue as to the direction the riders had taken. There were too many arroyos, low rocky outcrops and clumps of yucca for Wes to get a clear sighting; any of those features could hide a gang. But dust and disturbed ground, pockmarked with horseshoe impressions, deep at the front with loose dirt kicked out at the back, were a clear indication of several riders travelling at speed. Following his gut feeling that the riders were making for the mountain range east across the valley, Wes charged on as fast as his horse was willing to go. It was a fine quarter horse, Ned by name, and as gutsy as they come, but Wes knew he wouldn't be able to keep up for long. Without consciously being aware of anything in particular, senses can be heightened during a chase. The urgency, the excitement and the adrenaline all conspired to sharpen the sixth sense. Wes suddenly pulled up beside a yucca. The clouds of dust ahead had ceased to rise. A pair of cactus wrens shot up into the sky, startling him. Then the quiet of the morning was punctuated only with an occasional neigh and the tell-tale jingle of harness metal. The riders had stopped.

In the split second that Wes was alerted to the sudden change of events, and before he could complete his descent from the saddle, a single shot rang out, reverberating round the rocks and filling the air with a loud report. Half dismounted, Wes took the bullet in his thigh, knocking him to the ground. For a moment he thought he had simply slipped from the stirrup and fallen, the hard thud to the unforgiving ground overriding the pain of the wound. The shock of

24

the fall was momentary: the burning sensation in his leg became excruciating. He gripped his thigh and felt the wet stickiness of blood as it began to seep through his trousers. He could feel the torn edges of the material and, although he hated to explore further, he was relieved to find that the wound was mostly superficial and the long gash suggested the hot lead had not pen-etrated the muscle and was probably lying a distance away in the desert sand. But the pain increased with every moment. Wes quickly loosed his neckerchief, fumbled to get the torn material of his trousers away from the wet wound, pressed the necktie onto the ripped flesh and applied pressure. It was the best he could do. Unable to move with the shock of his injury, he gradually passed from daylight into black oblivion.

With flickering eyelids and a strange feeling of angels' arms around his shoulders, Wes imagined he was being raised into heaven. The light was very bright and he was weightless and serene.

'Easy there, fella.'

A water bottle was being pressed against his lips and he felt the cool liquid dribbling down his chin. His eyes wouldn't focus properly but the angels seemed much darker than white, and the hands felt a lot rougher than the delicate skin of an angel.

'What . . .' but the water stopped any more words and he tried to swallow as best as he could. Gradually, more of the world began to come into focus. There were two or three men standing and someone leaning over him.

'You've taken a hit in the leg, son. Lucky we came this way or you'd have baked to a biscuit out here. You're Wes Vernon, aren't you? Crazy fool that hared off like a jackrabbit after the robbers. I told you to wait.'

Feebly, Wes felt scolded. 'Sorry, Sheriff, but I thought . . .'

Josiah Fuller, one of the town's important merchants, stepped forward. 'Come on, Sam; let's get him back to town. The robbers have made good their escape for now. If they're prepared to shoot a man down, we'll need more than just the three of us to catch the sonsofbitches.'

A quick bandage was tied round Wes's leg, although the bleeding had all but stopped, being arrested partially by his own efforts. Carefully, Sam Cottrell, Josiah Fuller and John Hagen, the town's gunsmith, the only three men who made up the posse, lifted Wes onto his horse, made sure he wouldn't fall off and together they began the ride back to Sweetspring.

By the time they ambled back into Main Street, the townspeople were gathered noisily around the bank, fearful that their money may not be safe. Although the bank guaranteed deposits and was part of a consortium with establishments in other towns, bank robberies sometimes were so devastating to reserves that the bank went into liquidation and left investors, traders, farmers and everyone who dared put their trust in such places well out of pocket and sometimes destitute.

Doc Willan was still attending to Charlie Dobson's wound when Wes was carried into his front room. Through into the surgery the doc and his wife were

26

working on Charlie. The bullet in Charlie's chest had crushed bone and lungs. The doc's wife was trying to calm the patient while her husband poked about with a surgical knife and tweezers to pull the squashed lead out without doing further damage. A tricky job, and the prospects for Charlie were not good. The patient had been dosed up with liquor and a piece of leather was clamped between his teeth but he was mostly out of consciousness. Wes was thankful he wasn't carrying a bullet in his leg.

Outside the bank, the crowd had moved on from queries and concerns about their money to a more general heated discussion about these events. It seemed that half the town had gathered for a public meeting and the other half was making their way to join them. Too many bad things were happening to Sweetspring. Sheriff Cottrell left Wes in the doc's surgery and came out to quell the rising temperature of debate. He grabbed a chair from inside the bank and placed it squarely in front of the crowd. He climbed up, and the meeting gave him the due deference an elected lawman deserved. For a moment the crowd was quiet with anticipation. Cottrell drew in a deep breath; he wasn't sure how to begin.

'Listen, folks, I guess you'll be wantin' answers, same as me. I've just chased across the desert after a bunch of rats who came into town early this morning, smashed their way into the bank, grabbed what they could, fired off a load of shots, hit Charlie real bad, and rode out. Young Wes Vernon was just riding into town and he chased off after them.' He paused for effect. 'I shouted

27

for him to wait, but he didn't. Now me, Josiah an' John have just found him in the desert, shot off his horse and left to die.' There was a sudden outpouring of murmured questions and concern. Cottrell raised his hands. 'He's gonna be fine; just a flesh wound, I think, but he might have been killed. A brave young man who knows what's right and what's wrong. Now all this follows on two more things. Yesterday Tor Gudrun's pay wagon was robbed. Two good men were shot to death and a third went missing. Then, last night, some of you were in the Grand Hotel when gunmen burst in shooting off lead all over the place and shouted out a warning.'

'We're ready for them!' someone shouted, followed by more voices of support.

Cottrell continued, 'Well, I'd advise you all to carry side-arms for the next few days. I don't think we've heard the last of this gang. For some reason they've picked on us real good. I ain't got nothin' more to say right now. Take care. They ain't goin' to ruin Sweetspring!'

The air was filled with the outbreak of instant applause and shouts of *hooray* from the crowd. Folk dispersed slowly, little groups of people huddled into conversation, tradesmen returned to their shops and Main Street resumed normal activity. Later that day, after he had been busy talking with a few important people, the sheriff pinned a notice outside his office advising the good folk of Sweetspring that the town council would hold a meeting after Sunday's church service to decide what should be done. While all that was going on, Wes was being cleaned up and stitched back together by Doc Willan. Luckily, his quick action in staunching the blood and getting the ragged edges of material away from the wound had prevented any chance of infection. The worst part was the removal of a few embedded threads that had been forced into the wound and sealed with dried blood. The injury itself would heal quite quickly without doing any permanent damage. What it had done was to strengthen Wesley Vernon's resolve in bringing that gang to justice.

On the next day, Sunday, Wes made sure he was sitting near the Mancinis. He wasn't allowed to sit with them, as that would have implied a relationship with Maddy that Harry Mancini would not countenance in church. But he was near enough to keep glancing at Maddy and enjoy mutual smiles secretly. If only he could get Maddy away from her pa, Wes knew she would be true to her heart and marry him. He loitered outside the church after the service, hoping to get a word or two with Maddy, but she was staying too close to her parents. He thought they might be sympathetic seeing him with a crutch to take the weight off his heavily bandaged leg, but somehow the formality of church put up a barrier between him and the Mancinis. Social standing was not something he could sweep away, even with a crutch.

It came as something of a surprise when the sheriff approached Wes. 'Young man, Wesley, I'd like you to join the council meeting, if you would. You may be able to tell us something about these robbers. In any case, I think the council wants to formally acknowledge your bravery in giving chase yesterday.'

Feeling honoured and forgetting the disappointment of no conversation with Maddy, Wes complied gladly and went with Sam Cottrell to the council meeting. It was held upstairs in a spacious room of the Grand Hotel. Wes looked round at the faces. He recognized several of the town's important people: the bank manager Herbert Grenfell, the gunsmith John Hagen, his employer Tor Gudrun, Josiah Fuller represented the town's traders, and as he was looking at three faces he didn't know, the door opened and Harry Mancini took his place at the head of the table. Wes was introduced to the three people he hadn't met before: the chief railroad surveyor, a representative of the cattle ranchers' association and the owner of the Grand Hotel. The cream of Sweetspring society sitting round the huge oval mahogany table, its highly polished top gleaming in the daylight, like the careers of the men sitting round it. Sitting on a side chair, Wes felt distinctly out of place. Harry Mancini stood up.

'Gentlemen, we know only too well why we've been called to this meeting. It seems our town is under some sort of threat from a bunch of hoodlums, and we need to take some action to calm the good citizens and ensure that our businesses can carry on as normal.'

Wes noted that the main thrust of the opening remarks and the main concern was about the business interests of the men who were sitting at the table.

'Before we get down to serious discussion, there's another small matter. I asked Sam to bring young Wesley Vernon across so we can thank him for his bravery and quick thinking yesterday, which unfortunately resulted in him receiving a gunshot wound to the leg. Please stand up, Wesley.'

The table was tapped gently by all the men and heads were nodded in sage agreement of Mancini's praise for the young man. Needless to say, Wes was more touched by the thanks because it came out of the mouth of Harry Mancini, the man he most wanted to impress. Notwithstanding the pain in his leg, Wesley stood up as bidden and the room fell silent, apparently waiting for him to speak.

Wes cleared his throat nervously. 'Well, as far as the robbery at the mine is concerned, Mr Gudrun here will tell you we couldn't do a darned thing. A gun was being held to his head. Three men dead an' all. I believed he would have been shot too, if we'd tried anything. As for yesterday, I was riding into town quite early, comin' to see Sheriff Cottrell because I believed I had important information about the robbery at the mine, and also about the wild riders who shot at you folks in the Grand Hotel on Friday night.'

Herbert Grenfell interrupted. 'I still think someone tipped off the robbers about the bank being open early yesterday, because that isn't usual an' somebody must've known.'

'You knew,' said the sheriff, and a ripple of polite laughter went round the room. The sheriff turned to Wes. 'You were coming to see me?'

'Yes, sir, I was.' Then for some inexplicable reason, Wes suddenly stopped speaking. He was about to say what was on his mind, but something prevented him.

31

He looked round the table. Suppose someone had tipped off the robbers about the bank, maybe also about the exact timing of the wages wagon going to the mine; it was changed week to week to confuse any would-be robbers. Suppose that informer was one of these worthy men sitting here at this table? It seemed impossible, but Wes changed his next sentence knowing that to divulge his information might sign his own death warrant.

He did a double take and continued. 'What puzzled me was why riders at the mine came back so soon to shout that warning at the Grand Hotel and then attack the bank. I wondered why they'd do that.'

In fact he wondered nothing of the sort, and since the observation was very feeble, Mancini thanked Wes immediately for coming and suggested that he was now free to go. Wes took the hint and left the meeting. He was glad to get out into the fresh air. There had been an almost imperceptible change of atmosphere when the bank manager had suggested that an informer might be involved. The moment had evaporated in the room, but it had stopped Wes telling the members of the town council what was on his mind. The fact was that Wes was sure he knew the leader of the robber band. He'd grown up with him, been to school with him, played Civil War soldiers with him, and he'd have recognized his voice anywhere. It was Doyle Casey.

4

Back in the security of his own shack, Wes reflected on the strange meeting in the upper room of the Grand Hotel. Why had he felt that sudden reluctance to speak his mind? It was unlikely that any of the town council would know Doyle Casey. He poured himself a cup of coffee, rolled a smoke and sat out on the veranda. The sun was high, beyond its zenith but still burning hot and the veranda afforded some welcome shade. He blew a thin stream of blue smoke into the air. He was left with few alternatives and decided in that moment exactly what he had to do. There was only one person with whom he could share his plan safely, and she would have to be sworn to total secrecy as a matter of life and death. He would have a chance to talk to Maddy in the coming week. Tor Gudrun had told him to take some time off until his leg was completely healed, so nobody would miss him at work for a while. Tomorrow morning he would make a move.

Monday began the week with an unexpected cloud-burst. It lasted no more than five minutes, but in that time it turned Main Street into a riverbed, no more than an inch or two deep but right across the entire width, and running swiftly with the force of gravity on the gentle slope. Wes had just arrived at John Hagen's gun shop and hitched Ned to the rail when the rain started. Ned's head went down and his ears flopped as Wes went into the shop.

'Wesley Vernon! Local hero. Good day, young sir.'

'Good day to you, Mr Hagen.'

'Now, let me guess. Because of that robbery, you're looking for a significant handgun?'

'No, not especially. We don't carry guns in the mine; surely you know that. Just a trade-in. I'm just thinking of trading mine for a more recent model, single-action, but with some kick.'

John Hagen unlocked the counter cabinet and took out four revolvers one at a time and placed them carefully on the glass. He lined them up exactly in the same way, barrels at forty-five degrees off the vertical, almost exactly nine inches apart and grips towards the client, ready for them to pick up.

'Take hold of one, feel the balance. This is my favourite,' he said pointing to the Remington. 'The army model. It's a forty-four calibre. You won't find a better one than that.'

Wes picked it up. It was heavy. 'It's too big, Mr Hagen. Makes me look like a bounty hunter. I guess you could shoot a man's head off with this thing. Something with a shorter barrel.'

Hagen took two of the guns away and put three more on the counter. He pointed to each one. 'Smith and

34

Wesson, or this one's a handy little New Line revolver; it's a forty-one calibre rimfire, maybe too small. What about this beauty? That's what you should have.'

Again, it was much bigger than Wesley wanted, and he had an inbuilt distrust of any goods that were being pushed in his direction unless he was one hundred per cent sure of the seller. John Hagen was on the town council; in Wes's mind, none of them were to be trusted until the robberies had been resolved. The more he thought about it, the more he was convinced that someone important had to be pulling the puppet strings. If he could find the puppet, he would eventually be able to follow the string back to the manipulator.

'For myself, I rather like the look of this one. Can I try it?'

'Of course you can. A good weapon, a Smith and Wesson, but it's a thirty-eight. If you're thinking of buying a rifle as well – and maybe you'd have got a shot off at those robbers if you'd had a long range weapon – then you should go for a forty-four, then I can cut you a deal on a new Winchester that will use the same ammunition. There's a lot to be said for that. Just try this one.'

He handed Wesley a second-hand Colt forty-four. 'Now, step right this way.' Hagen led the way out to the back of the shop where there was a short firing range. He gave Wes six bullets. Wes loaded three and snapped the cylinder shut. He fired off two shots quickly, inspected the cylinder, squeezed in the three remaining shells and fired them more slowly, taking eyesight aim on two and then a hip shot for the third and fourth.

'You've got yourself a deal, Mr Hagen,' he said.

That same day, despite the awkwardness of his bandaged leg, Wes rode out into the desert with a box of fifty shells. Finding a sheltered spot, he built a stack of stones about four feet high and placed a big heavy rock on top. Taking his time, he emptied the cartridge box from a variety of distances and a variety of positions standing, turning and running, half with the second-hand Colt revolver and half with the new Winchester. When he checked, the heavy rock had taken a number of hits, not enough to shatter it, but plenty of pock marks. Equivocal about his shooting accuracy, he rode home well pleased with his purchases, despite the hole it made in his savings for the hoped-for wedding with Maddy. And thinking of Maddy, he was going to see her on the next day in the afternoon. That's when he would tell her what he was planning.

Tuesday morning, Wes was up early. There were things to be done. He swung himself out of bed, keeping his injured leg straight – not that he had any choice about that as it was heavily strapped with a short splint to prevent the stitches being pulled apart accidentally, especially during the night. Being fit, young and healthy, it wouldn't take long to heal. He saddled Ned and rode into Sweetspring for some supplies, hitching up outside Josiah Fuller's dry goods store. There was already a small group of customers. Wes waited patiently for his turn.

'Good morning, Mr Vernon. How's the leg?' Fuller

said politely. 'What are you needing today? Flour, salt, sugar?'

'Yes, all of those. Ten pounds of flour, one of sugar, a packet of salt, a tin of coffee, ten pounds of dried beans, a large box of easy-strike matches and a pack of smoking tobacco.'

'One at a time, young sir,' Fuller said as he went from shelf to shelf. Eventually all the things were gathered and Wes handed over the cash. Fuller put in an extra pound of beans on account that Wes paid cash as opposed to asking for credit like so many of the town's inhabitants.

'That should last you a couple of weeks,' Fuller said by way of conversation, not realizing that was exactly what Wes had calculated for his imminent journey, about which, of course, he said nothing. His next port of call was the butcher, from whom he purchased a lump of cured bacon. With the essentials in his saddle-bag he made his way back to his shack. A light breeze swept across the road, swirling the dust and propelling tumbleweed to a far away destination. Somewhere there must be a huge mountain of gathered tumbleweed.

Wes spruced himself up for the afternoon rendezvous with Maddy. It was a meeting he was looking forward to with some trepidation. He was always excited about seeing her, but there was the anxiety over her pa's domination and he had already banned Maddy from seeing Wes, especially now there was talk of the suitor from Boston. But Wes was also concerned about Maddy's reaction when he let her know that he was going away for a while. It was important that someone knew what he was doing, and Maddy was the only person he could trust. Even Tor Gudrun could be the source of information for the robber gang – most unlikely, but Wes wasn't going to take any chances whatsoever.

On Tuesday afternoons, Maddy and her chaperone would usually ride out to a particular spot near a clump of willows and a water hole that sometimes actually had water in it and became a short stream going from nowhere to nowhere. It was Maddy's favourite spot in the desert. Birds would come down to catch insects, occasionally to drink, and small animals were sometimes seen if the watchers were patient and quiet. A snake might sometimes appear looking for a meal. Wes took his time to ride out there. The roughly marked track meandered its way through the low mesquite bushes, the gaunt yucca and the cleverly spaced creosote, each in its own territorial watering space. He was savouring the thought of a meeting with his beloved girl. The chaperone, one of the maidservants, was the soul of discretion and never encroached within hearing distance. Wes could practise all his soft talk on Maddy and woo her with gentle words and kind gestures without fear of rebuke. It wasn't very often he could get away from the mine to have private chats with Maddy during the day. His injury was welcome on that account for the time it was giving him away from work.

Dismounting, Wes found a boulder to sit on and scuffed the dirt gently with his boot. The waterhole actually had some water in it from the recent rain; he was amazed at the wildlife that it attracted. Engrossed in his observations he hardly noticed the passing of time; it was surely time for Maddy to turn up. He got up and walked onto a rocky outcrop to look back down the valley. Two riders were making their way along the track. He guessed it was Maddy and her companion. He jumped down and went back to wait. Shortly Maddy and the maid rode into sight. Maddy pulled up and jumped down. She ran into Wes's arms and stayed still for a while, hugging him close.

'Oh, Wes,' she said, 'Father has forbidden me to see you. The man from Boston is already travelling by train and stage, and I've had to promise not to see you again for dances or anything. I can't stay here now, if he knew I was with you I would be confined to the house.' Tears streamed down her face, her eyes were red with crying. 'What am I to do?'

Wes took her face in his two hands and looked into her eyes. He kissed her. 'You must do as your pa says, Maddy. Just don't promise to marry the stranger.'

'I'll try not to,' she said and, in her distress, pulled away sharply and mounted her horse. With unseemly haste she took the reins, kicked the flanks and looking over her shoulder, shouted again, 'I'll try not to!'

In a moment, dust was all that was left of their meeting. Wes was in a daze; it had all been so sudden. And then he realized he hadn't told her his plan. Nobody would know what he was going to do. Did it matter? It wouldn't have to; he'd have to hope that things turned out all right. It wasn't his safety that bothered him now, but the pressure that would be put on Maddy to become betrothed to this interloper from

Boston. Well, one thing was sure: the robbers would come first, and then he'd deal with rich Mr Bostonian.

Wes went back to the watercourse and its muddy water. It reflected his mood: everything at the moment was unclear. For no good reason he tossed a small stone into the middle. It made little noise and he watched the ripples spread slowly to the edge. Philosophically, he said to himself that small actions could have large consequences.

He unhitched Ned. 'Consequences, Ned. That means things that follow on. You do something and all sorts of things happen because of it. We're going on a journey, me and you. A sort of mission. I want to look up an old acquaintance. What do you say to that?'

Ned snorted at the appropriate moment; Wes would've liked to know what he was thinking. He gave the horse a jab in the ribs and they trotted back down the track. Tonight he would have to get everything together so they could set off just before sun-up next morning.

5

Before dawn, the desert is a cold place. Hardly anything moves without the heat of the sun, there are few early morning hunters. Wes was the exception. He break-fasted on some scraps left over from last night's meal, accompanied by good fresh coffee. Then he loaded up Ned with his essential supplies and set off into the wilderness long before the sun had begun to come up from the other side of the world. There was no new horse furniture; having checked the state of the reins, the stirrup leathers and the cinch, everything was in good repair. The only new addition was a saddle holster for the Winchester. The only supplies that hadn't been bought in town were a dozen sticks of dynamite that had come from the mine.

Riding out into the half-light of the desert night, Wes felt a strange sense of adventure come over him. Here he was, stealing away from the environs of Sweetspring like a surreptitious fugitive, armed to the teeth with powerful weaponry, astride a sure-footed and fleet quarter horse with enough supplies to last for a good fortnight. He felt like an early pioneer searching for a

41

pass across a mountain range. Luckily, the pass that Wes was headed for had been discovered a long time ago. It would take him over the range into the next valley and then eventually to the bustling township of Coldbush, where he had grown up and gone to school with Doyle Casey.

The desert landscape abounds in water-cut and wind-blown features, sometimes hidden by random handfuls of tenacious vegetation. Away from the main route, what looks like a track may just be a dried watercourse. When the sun is up, strong shadows make it a deceptive place. At night, travellers are lost easily, and were it not for the relative flatness of the valleys and highly visible mountain ranges, they could wander aimlessly for days and die of thirst. For that reason, few honest people travel off the road at night, and Wes kept to the main way well marked with the wheels of carriers' wagons, the twice-weekly stagecoach and a good number of galloping horses.

The early morning sun cast long shadows as it lit the sky with gold, then yellow, and finally a cloudless blue. A long day lay ahead and, with a bit of luck, just one overnight stop would get him within reach of Coldbush. Deep in thought about how he was going to find his childhood friend Doyle Casey, Wes hadn't noticed that he attracted the attention of another rider who was following him a few furlongs behind. It wasn't until the stranger caught up and spoke that Wes became aware of him. The man came alongside.

'Howdy, traveller! Guess we're going the same way,' he said jovially.

Wes turned in the saddle to look at him. He didn't like the look of the unshaven face and the greasy locks of hair peeking under the hat. The man's cheeks were hollow, and as he smiled at Wes his few remaining teeth shone yellow and black. His speech was a little slurred and his breath stank of booze. His gun-belt was stuffed with shells, but he didn't look as if he was a particular threat. It was a practised nonchalance and Wes was put off his guard.

'Howdy,' Wes replied.

'Let's ride together. Always safer to travel with others, I always say. Roads out here can be lonely. Plenty of bad people about, vagrants, ridge riders and the like.'

Wes didn't notice another rider a short distance behind on his blind side. 'We don't see too many shifties round here, glad to say. You riding a grub line? You're not from these parts, are you?'

'No, sonny, I ain't. I'm just here to do a bit of robbery.'

The comment was so unexpected that Wes laughed out loud. 'Not much to rob round here.'

'No, there ain't. That sure is right. The desert's an empty place. But I'll take that shiny new Winchester.'

Wes thought he was joking. 'I don't think so.'

'Well, it's like this, sonny. Either you hand it over, and be robbed, or my partner will drill one massive hole in your back and you'll be robbed and shot. You choose, sonny.'

Wes pulled up sharply. The fact that the toothy man hadn't tried to pull a gun made Wes look behind and he saw the man's partner with a shotgun pointing directly at him. One blast from that would pepper both himself and Ned, and he wouldn't know anything about it. Smartly, Wes made a decision. It was a gamble; he was thinking he'd probably be shot anyway. He reached forward to unsheathe the Winchester. Calmly, and trying to appear relaxed, but keeping one eye firmly on the man's hands, he gripped the rifle.

'All right, I'll give it to you. But you'll probably shoot me, anyways.'

'No need for that kinda talk, young'un. We're honest robbers, not murderers. Murder brings out a posse and judges and hanging committees. But if you hand over your rifle, and maybe anything else, who cares much? Only you, and you've got too much sense to value a gun above your life. Ain't that so? Just hand it over an' we'll be on our way. Now take that gun out real careful. No fingers on any triggers. Know what I mean, sonny?'

Wes pretended to pull the Winchester from the holster, but it was stuck. He tugged. 'It's a new holster,' he said to the man. 'I only got it yesterday with the gun. It's not the best fit. Very tight.' He tugged at it again.

'Easy there,' said the man, 'let me see.' He started to move his horse towards Wes.

Wes had cleverly managed to ease his hand far enough into the top of the holster with the pretended pulling to get his hand forward of the stock and a finger on the trigger. At the same time he had slipped both feet out of the stirrups slowly. His heart was thumping in his chest; he would only get one chance and the odds were heavily against him.

He pulled the trigger. There was a loud bang as the

Winchester fired a bullet through the end of the holster into the dirt. Confusion followed. Ned was startled and bucked. Wes fell off, exactly as he had planned, shielded by the horse. He pulled his six-gun as he fell and fired a shot towards the man with the shotgun immediately. It missed, but his horse reared and, as it came down, the second shot struck the man in the chest and knocked him clean out of the saddle.

'Stop!' shouted the toothy man. 'That's enough.' He fired a shot underneath Ned at Wes's boots, but only the sand shuddered. 'We can stand here an' kill each other, or you can let me tend my partner and we all ride away an' forget this ever happened. What do you say?'

'I say help your friend, get on your horses and clear out.' One robber was prostrate in the dirt, the other hiding behind his horse, and Wes was uninjured so far. It was the best outcome Wes could hope for.

'Listen, sonny. We didn't mean you no harm. Matter of fact, we was going to invite you to join us. Make a small band, working with some local inside informa-tion. What do you say?'

'I say the sooner you clear out, the better.'

Toothy started moving towards his friend. 'No need to be unfriendly.'

His partner was writhing on the ground. It couldn't have been a chest hit or he would be stone cold dead. Sheltering behind Ned, Wes watched the other man retreat cautiously. In the tense standoff the injured man was helped onto his horse. Wes kept his trigger finger primed as he eyed the active robber, hoping he wouldn't take a shot at Ned. It was common to shoot a horse to

45

secure a getaway. For his part, Wes could have taken another shot at Toothy as he helped his partner, maybe killed them both and cleared up a couple of vermin. But it felt wrong to do that, too much like cold-blooded murder instead of justice, and Wes held off, glad to be unscathed by the encounter.

With his heart still thumping and blood pumping violently round his brain, Wes watched them go as they withdrew slowly, gradually getting into a canter as soon as they could. Wes was left trembling with delayed shock, half surprised that he was still alive. It was probably thanks to drink that the two robbers had been less than efficient in their intended action. They certainly weren't professional gunmen, and they had misjudged Wes, thinking he looked a bit of a greenhorn. Wes realized he needed to sharpen up if he was going to meet with Doyle Casey and carry out his plan. His hands were still shaking as he put bullets in the empty chambers and reflected on the way he'd handled the Colt. He turned it over in his hand, tried to spin it on his index finger and nearly dropped it. In a way he was glad he had missed the man on the horse. Even though they were a couple of no-goods, he didn't like the idea of killing out-of-hand. Judges and juries should carry the responsibility for dispensing justice, same as the duties of the sheriff and marshal: the rule of law had to override the rule of the gun.

Having crossed the mountain range into the next valley, the terrain was changing into a greener place where vegetation was more abundant; the distance was green rather than yellow, and trees more plentiful. It was altogether less inhospitable, at least in the landscape. Wes had to make an overnight stop in a dirty little hotel, which was no more than a hovel, where he ate some kind of indescribable steak for dinner, drank beer that tasted like brackish water and slept in his boots with his revolver in his hand. A decent cup of coffee for breakfast was its only saving grace and he was glad to get out on the road for another day of hard riding. Almost overwhelmed with memories of childhood, just before nightfall he pitched up in the outskirts of Coldbush. It was so much bigger now, quite a bustling junction where an east-west road crossed a busy valley trade route. This is where he hoped to get information about Doyle Casey that would lead him to the gang's hideout.

One of the things Wes remembered about Casey was that he was a home-loving kid, very insecure and always fearful that his pa was going to run out. As a child, Wes had been to the Caseys' ranch many times. He and Doyle had played endless games of hunting down Indians, or taking opposing sides in re-enactments of Civil War battles. He remembered when they'd dug miniature earthworks to represent Manassas Junction and placed wooden soldiers to defend the town, and threw pebbles to try and knock them down. Then, one day, Doyle's pa did run out. Nobody even knew what caused it. He just took off. Next thing they heard he was accused of robbery and murder, and was caught and hanged by vigilantes. Doyle never got over that. He swore vengeance and vowed never to leave his heartbroken ma. All that was a long time ago. But it strengthened the idea in Wes's mind that Doyle would likely be a regular visitor to his childhood home.

Wes hitched up outside Nooner's Saloon, one of the old original Coldbush buildings from the early settlement. Nooner was a friendly old guy who reputedly never got out of bed before midday, which gave him his nickname and settled his reputation. More than likely he was up and busy with saloon things out of sight somewhere, but the nickname stuck. Wes pushed through the batwings and approached the bar.

He called down the counter. 'Creosote, and make it quick!'

Nooner looked up. 'Creosote? You jokin'? Why . . . gracious me, is that you, Wesley? Young Wesley Vernon all growed up and started shaving! Dang me, you ain't been here for years. 'Bout the size of a jackrabbit last time I see'd you. Now look at you.' Nooner leaned over the counter. 'Carrying a powerful sidepiece, too. Guess you're drinking whiskey these days!'

'No, just a beer, you old fraud.'

Nooner pulled a glass of beer and slid it down the counter. Wes had to put his hand out to stop it flying off the end. Nooner walked down and leant one elbow lazily on the shiny polished mahogany top. 'Jes' testin' your reflexes! You need to be quick in this town these days. Things have changed since you left. Town's twice the size and attracts all sorts. You a bounty hunter now?'

Wes laughed out loud. 'No, sir, that I'm not.' But he paused and thought about it while he took a gulp of beer. How did Nooner see through him? Just a guess, or years of experience as a saloon owner summing up the

48

clientele? 'Matter of fact I've come back to look up an old buddy, my childhood friend Doyle Casey. You remember Doyle?'

'Sure I remember Doyle. Don't need to remember him; I see him from time to time.'

Wes tried not to hide his delight at that remark.

Nooner poured himself a whiskey. 'Yeah, you were both fightin' over the same girl at one time, pair of young bucks you were. Must've been ten year ago. Aimee: pretty girl. Aimee Vangraf. Her daddy owns the biggest bank in town, you know. And a regular stage-coach operation, not for passengers, for cash and valuables, Vangraf Express Co. Doyle worked for them for a while.'

'You're a mine of information, Nooner. How do you know so much stuff?'

Nooner tapped his nose. 'I jes' listen and serve the customers. Ain't nothin' to it. So what do you do these days, Wesley?'

'Mining. I'm an explosives man. A silver mine near Sweetspring, over the mountain.'

'Yeah, I know Sweetspring, never been there of course. A rowdy town I hear.'

'No, sir!' Wes was adamant. 'Nothing of the sort. A good, quiet, god-fearing place. Until recently, anyway. This last week we had two robberies and a shoot-up.'

'So what brings you to Coldbush? Is it Doyle Casey or are you really looking for Aimee Vangraf? You a married man, Wesley?'

Wes laughed again. 'No, sir!'

'And that limp you've got. A mining accident?'

49

'How did you notice that? Yes, nothing serious, luckily. Got hit by a piece of rock while blasting.'

'Well, you're welcome here any time Wes. Got to serve other customers. Nice talkin' to you.'

Nooner went off down the other end of the long counter. Wes took his beer and made himself comfortable at a table. He picked up a copy of the Coldbush Courier that was lying on the table and read some of the local news. It felt strange being back in his old town. On the front page there was a big advert for Vangraf Express extolling their virtues and saying how they'd never lost so much as a brass farthing of clients' shipments: the most trustworthy high-value carrier in the state, probably in the whole of the US. Every wagon was apparently protected by an armed guard of at least six men. Wes imagined Vangraf had made his wealth out of the war by confiscating shipments of supplies and money, enough to start up a bank when peace returned, anyway. Now it was the biggest bank in the town. Reading the advert made Wes think not of old man Vangraf, but of his beautiful daughter Aimee. Nooner was right, both he and Doyle had vied for her affection when they were about sixteen years old and Aimee was a stunning young girl with long shiny pigtails and dreamy doe eyes. Kid love, nothing came of it. The disappointment of rejection by Aimee one day was partly what made Wes move away. Lost in his reminiscences, Wes hadn't noticed other drinkers moving around the tables until he was approached.

'Mind if we sit here?'

Wes waved his hand in acquiescence. 'Sure.'

'Kind of you,' the man smiled and, as Wes looked up at him, showed a fine set of yellow and black teeth. 'No hard feelings, sonny?'

The two men sat down. Wes's hand dropped to his holster and he gripped the Colt without taking it out.

'No need for that,' Toothy rebuked. 'You made your point the other day. We've taken a shine to you. We're here recruiting.'

6

The two robbers of yesterday were the very last people Wes would have expected to come across within minutes of entering Nooner's Saloon in Coldbush. He was caught in a dilemma. His instinct was to march them off to the sheriff and lay a charge against them. At the same time he was mindful that he was quite lucky to have got away without injury in their last encounter, and he certainly didn't want a shootout in Nooner's Saloon. Then he remembered something Toothy had said.

Toothy smiled again and held out his hand. 'The name's Doug. This is my partner, Donel. Luckily he doesn't bear a grudge. You nearly winged him. He fell off his horse and I guess you thought you'd shot him. Say, you might like to buy us a drink?'

Buying drinks for robbers was the last thing Wes felt inclined to do, but he wanted some information. 'You're taking a bit of a risk, aren't you?' Wes said. 'I could just run you in to the sheriff.'

Doug and Donel smiled at him rather stupidly. Wes

concluded they hadn't many brain cells between them. Doug spoke up again, 'Listen, young'un. You could learn a lot from us. Why don't you join us? We're onto something big in a place called Sweetspring. Inside information, know what I mean?'

'A life of crime?' Wes exclaimed. 'I might be interested. Are you sayin' you've got a contact in Sweetspring?' Maybe he could indeed learn a thing or two from these reprobates. 'Nooner! Send over a couple whiskeys!'

In the next hour of conversation, Wes kept his two guests well supplied with liquor to loosen their tongues. He had a hunch about why they were anxious to recruit a new member to their gang of two. Once they were sufficiently boozed up to present no danger, Wes began some detailed questioning.

'So you were with a bigger outfit?' he guessed.

Doug looked at Donel and laughed. 'What do you say, Donel? Bigger outfit? Was that slimebag head of a bigger outfit?'

Donel spoke for the first time. 'Bigger when we were in it!'

'You had a disagreement?' Wes wondered.

'Big time,' replied Doug. 'We'd staked out a shipment. Have you heard of the Vangraf Express Co? Big noise round here, Vangraf. Well, he brags about the protection of his wagons, but Donel here heard about a short order bullion transfer that wouldn't get the full guard 'cos they were out on the reg'lar coach. So we tells Casey this and he says no, to leave it alone. That was sheer crazy. We said we were going to have a go. He said if we did, not to come back to his outfit. Well, that was two months ago. We had a go at the wagon, held it up, got one of the cash boxes but more guards suddenly turned up. We was lucky to git away with our lives and just a bit o' cash. Bad show, really. We didn't dare go back to Casey.'

'Casey?' Wes queried casually. 'Who's that?'

'The big cheese. At least he thinks so. Just a crazed ridge rider with a doting band of hangers-on.'

'You sound bitter.'

'We're bitter, all right,' Donel added. 'If Casey and the rest had come with us, we'd have had them guards and all the loot.'

Wes wanted to probe, but was careful to remain disinterested. 'Why didn't he?'

'No idea. Spineless, I guess. Only ever wanted to do things he'd initiated. Know what I mean?'

'You mean he didn't trust you?'

'Yeah, that's about it. So we split. And now we're recruiting for our own outfit. 'Bout two months ago we done some cattle rustlin' down Sweetspring, a hold-up or two. We get tip offs from a businessman and he gets a share of the proceeds. Interested?'

Wes put on a show of fake curiosity. 'We could join up, the three of us, do some stuff in Sweetspring and maybe run this Casey to ground. You know where his camp is?'

'Sure we do, but you'd have to be loco to take on Casey. He's well dug in more 'an a day's ride from here.'

Wes had to keep feigning interest to get the information he wanted. 'That'd be toward the High Top range, I guess?'

Doug nodded, 'Yeah, right. Two Trees Hollow, it's called, two big ol' pines stripped bare by lightning. Gaunt and menacing, just like Casey himself.' They both laughed. Wes joined in for a different reason: *jackpot!*

Jackpot indeed. And acquired in such a strange way. They say God moves in a mysterious way, but this was beyond all understanding. There was one more thing Wes wanted to know.

'Who's your business contact in Sweetspring?'

Toothy grinned. 'You'll have to join us to know that.'

Wes stood up. 'Look, boys, I would, but I've got a wife an' all back home. I couldn't run out on her. Anyways, I'm turning in for the night. Good to chat, an' if we meet again, no shooting, eh!'

Wes took his leave, said goodnight to Nooner at the bar and left the saloon. It was dark outside and he hadn't checked into any hotel. He mounted Ned and rode on into the town centre, put Ned into livery and took a room in the first hotel he came across. He was tired but elated with the information that had dropped into his lap. Tomorrow would be the start of the next step in his hunt for Doyle Casey.

Breakfasting on steak and eggs, Wes was set up for the day's ride. Good hot coffee would keep the chill air of the morning at bay. He whistled as he walked along to the livery, saddled Ned and rode out in an easterly direction towards the rising sun and the High Top range. Those particular jagged peaks, which formed the backbone of the High Top, were right now edged in a pale streak of gold put there by the sun to announce that it was about to come over the top and flood the valley with a wave of light. A clock in the town struck six, and Wes was already on his way. Suspicious of coincidence as he rode out of Coldbush, he reflected on the good fortune that had given him his first real lead toward finding Doyle Casey. Suppose somehow Doug and Donel, two prize misfits, had known that he was looking for Casey; suppose they'd been sent to sound him out; suppose they'd deliberately given him false information. Impossible: nobody could have known what he was up to. He'd confided in nobody, not even in Maddy, although he had meant to.

Then, more seriously, he wondered how he was going to get into Doyle's hideout, and if a place called Two Trees actually existed. There would be guards, lookouts and maybe booby traps. The more he thought about it, the more it seemed like a ridiculously simple plan that was bound to fail. But how else could he make contact with Casey and not look like a bounty hunter? He decided the only way would be to see if he could locate Two Trees and stake out the place to check any activity. He'd got his supplies; he had everything he needed to camp out for a couple weeks if need be. So, starting his ride eastwards as the sun came over the High Top peaks, Wes had made his decision and prepared himself for a long day's trek towards the hazy purple outline of the distant mountains.

Ned plodded his way along ill-defined tracks, crisscrossed with cattle trails and short-lived pathways, which petered out amongst the tufts of grass and low-lying bushes. Occasionally a watercourse gave rise to abundant verdure with fair-sized trees and dense thickets. Within sight of such an oasis, Wes was thinking he should have delivered Doug and Donel to the sheriff to rid the highways and byways of such low vermin, when suddenly his thoughts were cut short by a strange sight. At first glance it appeared to be something like a pile of old clothes, but as he got nearer the clothes took on a form, and it was soon apparent the form was a human body, lying quite still. Wes approached cautiously.

'Hey there, buddy, you all right?' he called from a short distance away. 'Are you asleep?'

There was no reply, so Wes urged Ned forward a few steps, near enough to be surprised by a faint groaning. Taking no chances, Wes drew his Colt and slipped off Ned. He circled the body to check there were no obvious signs of weapons at the ready or that it might be a trap. He glanced all round in case there were other people about, but the brushwood was too thick to see into. There were very few discernible footprints, just some that most probably belonged to the man prostrate on the ground. Kneeling down at a safe distance, Wes spoke softly.

'Are you injured, fella? Do you need help?'

The man's eyelids flickered and a nasty grin curled the corner of his mouth before his face screwed up. 'Water,' he said very quietly. 'Water.' Instantly Wes knew he'd been lured into a dangerous situation but his instinct kicked in too late. The voice behind him was slow and measured.

'Nice an' easy, Wes. No quick movements. I won't be so soft this time.'

The voice was unmistakeable. The face of the man on the ground would have been too, except that somehow the brain doesn't always make the connections when the environment is different and it is not expecting to see people it knew from some other place. There were, of course, only two people who knew that Wes would be riding out this way at this time of day. This trap could be fatal.

The brain is a strange thing. Wes's brain had failed to make the obvious connection until it was too late; it had failed to identify Donel lying on the ground. It had, of course, recognized Doug as soon as he spoke, but as an early warning system Wes's brain had utterly failed him. However, another part of the brain was fully alert to the current situation and pressed Wes into sudden and precipitous action. He swung round and fired wildly in the general direction that he believed the voice had come from.

There was an immediate scream as Doug flew back into the ground, clutching his side, his six-gun spiralling into the air. Wes turned instantly back to the man on the floor and kicked him over to see what weapon he had. A revolver came into view, so Wes stamped on his hand with such force he felt the fingers crushing beneath his boot. Taking no further chances in the heat of the moment, he fired a shot into Donel's right hand. The man passed out with shock. Wes, too, was taken aback at his ability to commit gratuitous violence and wound a man who was already down on the ground, but with plenty of justification, since neither Doug nor Donel would have hesitated to slug him. He then turned his attention to Doug, who was squirming on his back, his hand pressed into his side where a red patch was spreading through his shirt. Carefully, he moved Doug's hand to inspect the wound. It was a nasty red gash, and because of the close range the bullet had passed clean though and blood was issuing from front and back. Wes eased himself round so he could keep an eye on Donel in case he wanted to cause more trouble when he regained consciousness. Wes loosened Doug's neckerchief and pressed it onto the ragged exit wound.

'You're gonna have to hold in there, while I get you back to Coldbush.'

'No,' Doug said weakly but vehemently. 'I'm done for. I ain't gonna survive those two holes. My life's draining away. Weren't worth nothin' anyway.'

'Don't say that,' Wes rebuked. 'All life is worth something.'

Satisfied that Donel was too traumatized to make any meaningful moves, Wes lifted Doug off the ground, dragged him to his horse tied up in the thicket and somehow heaved the body across the saddle. Blood was still dripping, but there was a good chance if enough of it stayed in the body to keep Doug alive for the two or three miles back to town. Donel, fully restrained with ropes, had recovered his senses sufficiently, and the sorry band was soon making its way back along the road to Coldbush.

Entering Main Street, the party attracted some attention, and before long Wes was able to send for the sheriff and get directions to a doctor. A deputy arrived quickly and took charge of Doug, leading his horse towards the doctor's town surgery. Moments later, the sheriff arrived and relieved Wes of his second hostage.

It was late that morning – gone eleven o'clock before all the formalities were completed in the sheriff's office – and Wes was free to get on his way. There was the prospect of a small reward if it turned out that Doug and Donel were wanted men and that the circuit judge convicted them of any crimes. In his own mind, Wes wasn't bothered about the reward so much as letting the rule of law take its course. It was a shame he hadn't got the other name out of them, but now once again he was ready to take his own course, which had been disrupted violently by the two no-goods. What else could possibly get in the way of Wes's search for Doyle Casey?

7

Having lost too much of the day dealing with Doug and Donel, Wes made nowhere near as much progress toward High Top range as he hoped. By late afternoon he seemed to be no nearer the mountains because of the deception of distance across the open country. When the sun went down, darkness would arrive quickly. He decided it was time to find a suitable scrape in which to settle down for the night. He had enough water in his canteen not to worry about the dry state of the many arroyos. In fact, just such a gully would afford the best kind of shelter. He wandered a good way off the beaten track for added security and, finding a good crevice where he could be totally hidden from view, he dismounted. Taking his saddle, bedding and two full saddlebags off Ned met with the horse's approval. He neighed and kicked at the ground. Wes hobbled him and let him wander in search of tussock grass.

In a short space of time a small fire was going, water was in a tin can to boil for coffee and Wes was twisting rough dough round a stick to hang over the fire. A slice of cold smoked bacon and a hunk of cheese were laid out on a paper bag. He wasn't concerned about the small amount of smoke winding into the sky. This was a very lonely place. Snakes and maybe coyotes were more of a concern than human marauders. Sitting back against his saddle waiting for the water, Wes pulled on his tobacco and blew a stream of smoke into the air, almost enough to rival the fire. It was a deep and satis-fying exhalation that encapsulated his entire feelings about the day. He knew he should have brought those two wastrels to justice when he had the chance in Nooner's saloon, but as it turned out the right thing had been done in the end. Drunk and pretty feeble, those two hopeless cases hadn't really presented much of a problem for Wes, despite his limited practice with the Colt. After all, like any young man in this part of America, he'd been handling a gun for quite a few years. Because of his employment he was also an expert with explosives. Nevertheless, Casey and his gang would be an entirely different proposition. In their own stupid way Doug and Donel had provided Wes with the kind of wake-up warning he needed.

Sunrise saw the remnants of last night's fire sparked into life as Wes chucked on more dried material gath-ered from the gleanings amongst the scrub on the banks of the arroyo. Water was already beginning to agitate in the can, set down in the hot embers as the new fuel began to flare around it. Wes wouldn't mount up until coffee and a smoke had officially begun the day, just as no day could begin without the sun climbing in the sky. Anything else was unthinkable. Ned was getting restless: he wanted to be on the move and he'd already satisfied his own need for breakfast, clipping leaves from the vegetation mixed with mouthfuls of spiky grass.

On the move at last, Wes steered Ned out of the dried-up gully and back towards the main track. High Top range seemed no nearer today than it had yesterday, which was a little depressing. Half-heartedly he dug Ned in the ribs and encouraged him into a trot, but there was nothing to be gained by increasing the speed and Ned soon slowed down of his own accord. The ground was rising steadily on to a low plateau, sitting above the surrounding ravine-dotted plain, and from the top of the incline there was a good view of the distant mountain range. Some long way across the flat ground, a cloud of dust was rising discernibly from the roadway, probably the regular stagecoach hurrying on its way toward Coldbush. At some point it would speed past Wes.

Going down the further side of the low plateau, the progress of the stage could be surmised from the clouds of dust. Wes took little further interest, but the next time he looked up there was a great deal more dust and everything seemed to have come to a halt. There could be only two reasons for that. The best would be a breakdown caused by the shedding of a wheel or a broken axle and the worst would be a hold-up leading to robbery and possible murder. Seconds later the sound of several gunshots travelled the distance between Wes and the stagecoach, reaching his ears a good while after the stage seemed to have stopped. Even allowing for the difference between the time taken for light and sound to travel, when gunshots are heard well after a hold-up has begun, it usually means things have turned bad and people have lost their lives. Either a passenger had pulled a gun rashly, or the boozed-up robbers, high on adrenaline, had lost patience. In the worst case, the robbers would be leaving no witnesses. Wes was much too far away to do anything, not that he wanted to take on a bunch of outlaws, but he kicked Ned into action and was soon galloping towards the dust-marked location.

Some five hundred yards from where he guessed the stage would be, Wes left the main trackway to skirt the area and get an idea of what was going on. By now the dust had settled and there was an eerie silence: no horses, no shouting, not anyone calling for help. It seemed safe enough to approach. Still in the under-brush, Wes moved Ned slowly toward the road. He slid off quietly and looped the reins into a bush. Coming soon to a sufficient thinning of the brushwood, Wes's eyes alighted on a desperate scene of carnage. One horse was quite dead, ensnared in bits of harness and dangling traces. There were no other horses; they must either have run away or been stolen. The coach was lying on its side; the airside wheel was turning very slowly on its hub, the only moving thing that was left at the scene. The driver was lying awkwardly across the front rail. Wes didn't need to get nearer to see he was lifeless: one arm hung over the wooden rail, the hand red with blood still dripping from the limp fingers. Horrified by the scene, Wes stood quite still for a moment. Ned's harness jingled in the bush, a cardinal bird called its song and insects were buzzing in for a feast.

The stagecoach door was lying open to the sky. Wes climbed up on an axle and heaved himself onto the flat surface. He peered inside. There were two bodies: a man in a light overcoat, face up, sprawled across the full width, and underneath him what looked like a woman in a purple silk dress, crumpled up into the door space. A jumble of clothes emptied from the travellers' valises had been thrown in through the open door, partially covering them. Carefully, Wes manoeuvred himself into the compartment. He swung down onto the side, avoiding the bodies. The man had been shot in the chest, twice by the look of it. Wes felt the neck vein. It was without any pulse.

With some effort, he managed to fold the man's body away from the upper half of the woman. There was a good deal of blood on her dress, but no visible bullet holes. Wes reached down and put his hand on her neck. There was nothing. He moved his hand and pressed again. A response? Bending down as far as he could, he got his ear to the woman's mouth and listened. Poised in an ungainly position, he couldn't tell if the beating was the blood in his own ear veins magnified with the effort of listening, or if there was the faintest hint of warm breath issuing from her mouth. Desperate to be sure, Wes risked injury to the woman and lifted her up as best as he could. Her head flopped backwards and Wes thought she must be dead, but the flopping of the head revealed her smooth white-skinned neck and an unmistakeable pulse in the tightened neck vein. She was neither dead nor very old; in fact she seemed rather young with beautiful unblemished skin.

Frantic to get the young woman out of the coach to revive her, Wes heaved at the dead man's body to free her. Looking carefully, he determined that the blood on the woman's dress had in fact come from the man and not from her. Hoping she hadn't got any broken bones that might puncture a vital organ, Wes struggled to free her completely. Once in his arms, he puzzled how he might get her out of the sky-facing door. The woman was as limp as a rag doll and, although Wes had his arms encircling her slender body for support, he couldn't lift her at the same time. The situation was further complicated by her being of the female sex and Wes, even in this circumstance, had to be very careful where he placed his hands. Somehow he was going to hoist her up through the doorway. But God must have been smiling on him for his good deed, for at that very moment of indecision the lady suddenly came to life, but in her confusion she lashed out.

'Let go! Let me go! What do you think you're doing?'

It was as much as Wes could do to fend off the blows without letting the woman fall back down into the chaos of the overturned coach.

'Stop! Stop!' he shouted at her, while trying to grab her flailing arms. 'Ma'am, I'm tryin' to rescue you.' But in that moment she had passed again into unconsciousness.

Wes's dilemma continued a while longer, but with a

good deal of heaving, shoving and indecorous man-handling he finally managed to get himself and the young woman through the door space and into day-light. He laid the woman on her back on the side of the stage and wondered how he was to get her down to the ground. But once in the fresh air and sunshine, God smiled again and the woman's eyes flickered.

'Now, ma'am,' Wes said hastily, 'before you start thrashing around again, let me say you're now in safe hands. I've hauled you out of the stagecoach and will get you down to the ground in a moment. Just breathe deeply and stay calm. I'm here to help you, not to do you any harm. Is that clear, ma'am?'

The young woman's eyelids opened wide and Wes was struck by the intense blue of her eyes. She squinted, grimaced and tried to raise herself on one elbow, but the unfamiliar angle of the overturned coach and a sudden dizziness caused her to fall back down into a lying position. Wes put his hand under her head so she didn't choke.

'Do you feel any better, ma'am?' he asked hopefully.

'A little,' she said grudgingly. 'And stop calling me ma'am, it's miss.'

'I'm sorry, miss, with your gloves on I couldn't tell if you were wearing a wedding ring or anything. I thought it was more polite to call you ma'am. Maybe the man was your husband.'

'Well, now you know otherwise, you can call me miss.'

'My, you are in a difficult frame of mind. Do you have a name other than miss?'

'Not for you, no. Now get me down off here and I'll be on my way.'

Wes laughed out loud. She sure was a spunky young woman. He climbed down off the side of the coach and walked away to retrieve Ned from the bush. He expected to hear a scream of distress and a demand for help. But to his utter surprise as he looked back, the woman began to ease her way off the edge of the coach. Wes stopped still and watched as she dangled her leg over the side and tried to find a step of some sort on the underside. He couldn't help noticing her smart button-side shiny black boot as it weaved side-to-side, searching for a hold. He smiled to himself, admiring her plucki-ness, but then it all went wrong: she slipped. Her voluminous skirt was snagged on a bar and ripped with a loud tearing sound as she fell awkwardly into the dust. She looked like a pile of expensive garments, crumpled and discarded. Wes ran back to her. Ned would have to wait.

'Pride comes before a fall,' Wes dared to say. 'Anything broken, except your standoff attitude?'

'Just let me be,' she replied without looking up. It was obvious she was badly shaken and in some pain. She was trying to restore her dignity by hastily wrapping the yards of torn material over her beribboned cotton drawers – without much success. 'My ankle hurts, thanks to you.'

Wes had had enough of her rude independence. Ned needed his attention more than the young lady. He went back to the thicket and whispered some words of advice into Ned's ear about not taking too much notice of stuck-up, ungrateful young women. He led Ned out onto the roadway and mounted. He knew the young lady was watching him from the corner of her eye. He walked slowly past her, looked down, tipped his hat. 'Have a pleasant day, miss.'

Her face was a picture. 'You, sir, are a rat!'

Ned kept walking, encouraged by Wes's boot to make sure he didn't stop. Wes didn't look back.

'Stop! Stop at once! Stop I say!'

Wes stopped but he didn't look back. He said in a loud voice, 'If I remember, miss, the man who fell among thieves on his way from Jerusalem to Jericho was grateful to the Samaritan for the help that he received.' He walked on.

She shouted after him. 'I'm sorry.'

Wes stopped. Some humility at last. He turned Ned round and walked back. From his elevated position astride the horse he looked down at the young woman, not with compassion, but disdain.

She looked up. 'I'm sorry,' she repeated. 'You didn't have to stop here, did you? You could have left me in there to die.'

Compassion returned. Wes slid down off Ned and picked the young lady up. She couldn't put her weight on her injured ankle. He helped her to the side of the road and sat her on a good-sized boulder.

'You're a plucky young lady, miss, but you wouldn't last half an hour out here on your own. You do understand that, don't you?'

'I can look after myself you know. I've got a pocket pistol in my bag.'

'Well, you'd better find it, then. Because there are plenty of bad people in these parts riding the trails looking for robbery, violence or in your case something much worse.'

She looked away, embarrassed.

'Now, perhaps you'd like to tell me something about who was travelling in that coach, where you were headed and so on. An' I'll see if I can help you.'

They sat together for a long time while the young lady told Wes that there were three passengers in the coach that had come from Messuite travelling to Coldbush, Sweetspring and on westwards. She was on her way to Coldbush where her uncle had a ranch; one of the men, a businessman who was no longer at the scene, was going to Sweetspring, and the dead man in the coach was a prospector travelling to southern California.

'He was sure he was going to make his fortune,' she said wistfully.

'The good Lord saved him a lot of heartache then. Most prospectors now find nothing but dust. The days of the gold rush are long since gone.'

'Are you a prospector? How do you know about that?'

'I'm a mine engineer, miss. I work in a silver mine in Sweetspring. Explosives. Rock blasting.'

'Sweetspring is where that other man was going. He was a wealthy businessman, had enterprises back east. He told us all about the opportunities out here for making money. I think he said he owned a bank in New York or Boston. Somewhere on the east coast.'

'But he's not here now.'

'No. I wonder what happened to him.'

'Do you remember anything of the hold-up?'

'Not really. Lots of shouting and shooting.' She looked directly into Wes's eyes. 'What am I to do now? Is it far to Coldbush?'

'Too far to travel on your own. Anyway, you haven't got a horse or anything. I can't take you back to Coldbush, I'm going east.'

'Can you get my valise out of the coach? And there's my hand luggage too, a small bag and a jewellery box.'

Wes climbed back into the coach and rummaged amongst the debris of the hold-up and the discarding of unwanted goods. He managed to find the carpetbag with a few female clothes in it. He found the small handbag with a pocket pistol still inside, but there was no sign of the jewellery box. He searched in the man's jacket pockets to see if there was any identification, some papers or any clues to his name. But his search was disrupted by the sound of neighing, the stamping of hoofs and the unmistakeable noise of an agitated horse. Wes stuck his head out of the door hole just in time to see the young lady hoisting herself into Ned's saddle and kicking her shiny black boots into his flank. Amidst the flapping of ripped pink satin skirt, Ned took off in the direction of Coldbush and Wes could do nothing but stare in a state of sheer disbelief.

8

Wes immediately cupped his hands by his mouth and yelled at the top of his voice, 'Ned!' His choice of horse's name had been deliberate. When he acquired the young quarter horse he had trained it hard day and night, as anyone would. The name Ned can be called out with a long high note for the 'Ne' sound before concluding with the terminal 'd'. Part of the young horse's training had been to call Ned from an increasing distance and eventually from out of sight. That was four years ago, and now it really paid off for the first time. With immense satisfaction, Wes watched Ned come to a shuddering halt, turn round and race back to his owner. Wes drew his pistol.

'You've a lot to learn about these parts, miss. As a horse thief I could shoot you dead here and now.'

'But you won't.'

'I might if you don't get down, behave yourself and stop pretending you've got an injured ankle. What in hell did you hope to achieve?'

She dismounted and shrugged her shoulders.

Wes holstered his gun and handed over the valise. 'I trust you've got something decent to wear in there. I've got to get news of this hold-up to a law officer. Coldbush is two days away. What's back the way you've come from?'

'A small town about half a day back. Avondale, I think it was called.'

She went behind the coach and returned shortly, wearing a light blue silk skirt. It went well with the undamaged dark pink top.

'That's the direction I'm going anyway. Now, there's precious little room for you; you'll have to sit behind the saddle on my bedroll and just hold on as best as you can.'

Wes helped the young lady up behind the saddle. She made a bit of a meal of climbing over Ned's rump and straddling on the bedroll. Wes handed up the extra luggage then swung himself up, being careful not to kick the young lady.

'Since we're going to be travelling a while, my name's Wesley Vernon. What's yours, miss?'

'Alice,' was the curt reply.

'Well, Alice, I want you to tell me exactly what happened, as far as you remember it, while it's still fresh in your mind.'

For the next several miles, Alice recounted her memory of the events that led up to the stagecoach being chased by a wild band of no-goods, the driver being shot and the coach eventually skidding over on its side. The two men in the stage tried to climb out through the door. She lost consciousness at that point, but when it was quiet she came to with the dead man pinning her to the floor. That's all she could remember. Wes asked about the other man: what happened to him? She couldn't remember. He pressed her to try and visualize the scene in her mind. She said it was all very confusing. She remembered the man next to the driver firing a shotgun at the bandits and then falling off the coach. That was before the driver was shot. Inside the coach it was difficult to know exactly what was happening. Then she remembered that the other man got out first and there was a lot more shouting. The second man was getting out of the door when they shot him and he fell down on top of her.

Wes pondered on the information. As there was no sign of the third passenger, the three most likely explanations were, firstly, that he'd been shot and was lying at the roadside hidden from view; secondly that he had been in on the robbery and was part of the gang; or thirdly that if he was wealthy he might have pleaded for his life and been taken hostage for ransom. Wes hadn't carried out a detailed search of the area but dismissed the idea that he'd been shot, otherwise the body would have been near the coach. So he was either part of the gang or had been taken prisoner. As this passenger stagecoach didn't belong to Vangraf Express Co., the one thought that he couldn't set aside was the likelihood that the band of robbers was led by Doyle Casey, whose hideout was not that far away at High Top ridge.

It was while he was chewing that over that he remembered Doug had said that Casey wouldn't attack a Vangraf Express shipment. Why not? One possible reason was that he had some agreement with Vangraf. Maybe he was robbing for Vangraf: a bank is an easy way to hide the proceeds of robbery. Or maybe Vangraf was taking money for not turning Casey in. With his head spinning, the next couple of hours passed without a single word of conversation. Wes had almost forgotten he had a passenger. It was only when she put her arms right round him and he felt her head on his back that he became aware of her. He guessed she was still traumatized by the hold-up and now, overcome with nervous exhaustion, had fallen asleep for nature to begin its recovery.

It was late in the afternoon when Wes and his passenger arrived in the two-bit town of Avondale. The sheriff's office was no more than a rough-built shack that also housed a general store and an attorney's office. Alice climbed down first, then Wes. Ned was hitched to the rail. Wes pushed open the office door. A bell swung above his head and a man came forward from the back of the shop.

'Good day, sir. What d'ye need?'

Wes was about to say he was looking for the sheriff when he noticed the man was wearing a silver star. It suddenly became clear that this man was not just the sheriff, but the storekeeper and the attorney, all rolled into one rather old, wrinkled, sun-beaten, walnut of a man. As a sheriff he'd probably never drawn his gun. In fact he wasn't even carrying one.

'Well, now,' Wes began, 'I've come to report a robbery. The stage that passed through here this morning, with this young lady and two other passengers, has been ambushed on the road. Driver and shotgun killed as well as one of the male passengers. The other one is missing. Was it carrying anything valuable?'

The sheriff stroked his chin while he gave the question some thought. 'My, oh my. That is bad news.' He turned to Alice. 'At least you're safe, miss.'

She turned away as if it wasn't seemly for her to be seen talking to the old man.

'As it happens, there was valuable cargo on the coach,' the sheriff-storekeeper-attorney continued.

Wes guessed. 'Gold? Bullion? Bonds?'

'None of those. Not directly. But I happen to know a very wealthy man was on board. He stopped here for a night before getting that coach this morning. Told me he was looking for opportunities out west. Wanted to buy up this town; said he could make something of it and turn it into a big rail junction. 'Course I didn't believe a word of it. Not until he showed me a small valise stuffed full of twenty-dollar bills. He said to me, "How much? How much would it take to buy up this town and surrounding land?" 'Course he was speaking to me in my capacity as an attorney. I told him I'd sound out some of the residents. He said he'd give me a week. He was off to Sweetspring for some pleasant business first.'

Wes's ears perked up. 'Sweetspring? What sort of pleasant business?'

The sheriff tapped the side of his nose. 'Said it was about some important partnership with a real nice bonus thrown in. Anyways, you say he's missing?'

'Yes. Did you talk to anyone about his bagful of money?'

The drift of the question was not lost on the sheriff; old he may have been but he wasn't senile. 'Not exactly, but you're thinking the same as me.'

Wes pursed his lips and nodded. 'Do you know Doyle Casey?'

'That vermin!'

'Do you know where I might find him?'

'Near Two Trees, up on the ridge. But I'd advise against it, unless you're tired of living. There's five or six of them up there, maybe more.'

'Did you know two ridge riders called Doug and Donel?'

'Yes, sir, I do.'

'Well, I killed one and delivered the other to the sheriff in Coldbush.'

'Are you a bounty hunter?'

'I didn't think so.'

The sheriff stroked his chin again; the bristles were probably itching. 'There's a reward out for Casey and his gang . . .'

'I'm not out for any reward. Me and Casey went to school together. I was wanting to look him up. Time to renew our friendship. Does that bother you?'

'Me? No, sonny, not in the least. You do what you want, so long as it leaves this little patch of God's earth in peace.'

'Good. Now, this young lady is going to need somewhere to stay.'

Alice swung round. 'Not in this wilderness,' she said vehemently. 'You rescued me, Mr Vernon. Now you must find me somewhere to stay.'

'That's easily done,' Wes said, turning away and hiding a smile with great difficulty.

They took their leave of the old boy – sheriff, store-keeper and attorney – and remounted Ned. With two up, Wes's baggage and Alice's as well, Ned was well laden and looked almost like a mobile fly-by-night trader's store. Wes led him off in the direction of the High Top range. He said over his shoulder, 'Hold on tight, miss. We need to make some progress before nightfall.'

It was a good quarter hour of steady cantering, inter-spersed with recovering walks, before Alice tapped Wes on the shoulder. 'You said you'd find me somewhere to stay,' she whined in a disgruntled voice.

'I will.' He paused. 'But only if you're willing to play the part of my wife.'

'I will not,' she said with utter surprise. 'I will do no such thing.'

Wes pulled up. 'Then you better get off now.'

'Out here, in the middle of nowhere! Why, you're no better than the worst of the robbers. You just see me as an easy target. Just a plaything, like most men think, just something to use as they wish, just . . .'

There was a loud bang as Wes fired a shot into the air.

'Alice, you whine real good. You're soundin' a lot like a wife already! Now hush up, an' when we get to camp I'll tell you what you've got to do.'

Before nightfall, Wes had made a good fire, boiled some beans, cut some bacon, brewed some coffee and laid out his bedroll. Seeing she had no alternative but to play along with Wes, Alice had relaxed a little and they sat together chatting while Wes had a smoke. She seemed unduly concerned about Wes's safety.

'Why do you really want to find this Casey person? If he's as dangerous as people say, what makes you think you might not get shot before he knows who you are? You can't just creep up on outlaws that easily, can you? Maybe you are a bounty hunter for all I know.'

'No, I'm just an explosives foreman at a silver mine, like I said. Why shouldn't I want to look up an old friend?'

'Something must have made you suddenly think about it. Have you left your work at the mine?'

'No. As a matter of fact, I got shot in the leg and so I've got time off. I thought I'd visit my old buddy.'

Alice was not convinced. She asked Wes to show her the wound if it wouldn't be embarrassing for her to see it. Wes duly lowered his trousers and let her feel the bandage over his longjohns. 'Ah, gently,' he said as she ran her hand over the strapping. 'It's still mending.' Then, remembering all that had happened to Alice that day, Wes told her to get into the bedroll and catch up on more sleep.

'So, where are you going to sleep, Mr Vernon?'

'I won't be sleeping, miss. I'll sit by the fire and doze.'

Alice pondered a moment. 'But you said I had to play the part of. . . .'

'Not like that, miss. I'll let you know when the time comes.'

Before settling down for the night, Wes mixed up

some flour and water in a can and left it open to the air overnight. By the morning it would be a good sourdough mix.

The cold desert dawn inveigled Alice's bedroll before sunrise. Wes saw her stirring and immediately put more brushwood on the fire to bring it into flames. Although he'd been cold in the night it hadn't stopped him falling asleep. Resting his head against his saddle and covering himself with the slightly short saddle cloth had given him just enough personal warmth to drift in and out of sleep, finally dropping into deeper slumber for a couple of hours. A degree of excitement in anticipation of reaching the so-called Two Trees location filled Wes with a sense of purpose. Hot coffee and a smoke reinforced the feeling well before Alice finally emerged from her unconscious state. Wes had cooked a piece of sourdough flatbread on a hot stone for breakfast. Alice complained of not having any fresh water to wash in. But feeling entirely helpless in such an unfamiliar situation she did reluctantly accept the warm bread and some coffee.

'I'm hoping we'll reach Two Trees today,' Wes announced brightly. 'If we do it could be dangerous. With you, I will look less like a bounty hunter and more like a lost traveller. It should be enough to save us from being shot.'

'Save you, you mean. Why would they want to shoot me? Women aren't bounty hunters.'

'Anyways, just do as you're told and when we do make contact with anyone, that's when you have to pretend to be my wife. We're just two prospectors who've gotten lost and are looking for help. Got it?'

'Prospectors? Without shovels and pans?'

'Have you got a better idea?'

Nothing more was said until they were packed, loaded up and on their way. Wes wondered whether he should ditch most of the supplies, which were quite a burden for Ned, and it seemed he wasn't going to have to camp out now that he had a good alibi for just riding into the hideout like a pair of lost fools. Once Doyle knew who he was, everything would be all right for sure.

By midday, Wes, Alice and Ned had reached the lower slopes of the High Top range. The overhead sunlight was throwing the rugged sides into sharp three dimensions with precious little shadow except dark vertical slices of deep purple. The outcrops were tall and sharp. Peering ahead, Wes discerned a winding track ascending through the sparse and stunted pines, sometimes in full view, sometimes hidden for a while, to emerge higher up the slopes. There was no chance of finding a way over the top; the skyline was a completely jagged rash of sharply serrated rock, the kind that, Wes knew from experience, didn't break into blocks but shattered into spear-like shards. The action of water and ice over the centuries had broken off chunks of sharp debris and gravity had deposited them as an almost impenetrable barrier at the foot of the mountain. It was prime terrain for big horn and such sure-footed creatures, and good hunting territory for mountain lions. A good place, too, for outlaws to make their home. Wes scanned for any sign of two tall burnt-out trees, but nothing matched the description. Urging Ned to be careful, Wes steered him to the base of the only track that he could be sure would lead him up the scarp.

They hadn't travelled more than half an hour, emerging from the first and lowest clump of sparse pines, when the singing of a bullet passed very close by and struck a tree, accompanied by the sound of the gunshot that had fired it.

'Good,' said Wes. 'I think we've been seen.'

'Good!' Alice shouted in alarm. 'That's good?'

Wes had a large white handkerchief at the ready, well prepared for this moment. He raised his arm high in the air and waved the makeshift flag from side to side. There was no more gunfire. Gingerly, he pressed his heels gently into Ned's sides and urged him forward at a walking pace. Scanning the mountainside all the time, Wes could make out nothing that looked like a human form. He pressed on.

Emerging again from the sparse cover afforded by some dotted pines, the same thing happened again. A shot was fired and Wes waved his flag. He was fairly sure the shots were not meant to hit him, just meant to be warnings. Otherwise someone was a pretty bad shot with their rifle. Then, suddenly, two figures on horseback appeared halfway up the scree, where Wes hadn't even noticed a track. He saw the fabled two trees at the same time that the riders came into view. He put his hand behind him and patted Alice on the thigh.

'Nothing hurried. Don't say or do anything. Let me do the talking and everything will be all right.'

The two riders came sure-footed down the track. It

took some five minutes for them to make the descent. Once off the steep incline, they approached quickly with handguns drawn. Wes was holding Ned with knee pressure only, his hands raised high in the air and still holding the handkerchief.

The first rider came right up to Ned and looked closely at Wes. He lifted the Colt out of Wes's holster and stuck it in his own gun-belt, and then he took the Winchester out of the saddle scabbard and laid it across his lap. He poked at the baggage and then felt Wes's boots for a secreted knife or pistol.

'A bounty hunter,' he announced. Then, looking at his passenger, 'Well, well, look here! Hello, Alice.'

9

The first rider continued to circle Wes and Alice. He had the audacity to lift Alice's skirt above her ankle, saying he needed to feel her boot for a concealed weapon, but his hand strayed off the top of her boot onto her leg. Alice swept his arm away with a sharp downward movement. The two outlaws laughed.

The man pretended to be shocked. He was twitching with excess adrenaline. 'She's got a bit of fire! Now, do we shoot this bounty hunter here and now?'

Wes knew his life was in the balance, but on the spur of the moment, Alice spoke up. 'I don't think Mr Casey would thank you for killing his friend.'

The man laughed a silly high-pitched noise 'Oh, he's a friend is he? Not a bounty hunter, then? What's your name, sonny?'

'Wesley Vernon. Doyle and I went to school together in Coldbush, so kindly take us to see him. He'll be grateful.'

'Grateful, eh?' he mimicked Wes, 'What do you think

about that, Davey? Is he telling the truth?' The rider drew his gun and cocked it.

Davey offered his opinion. 'Best not to shoot him, Kyle, in case he is Doyle's friend.'

Kyle smiled unpleasantly and waved his gun towards Wes. 'That's lucky, Wesley. For the moment, you live. Now follow us.' A silly high-pitched laugh again.

The two outlaws, Davey and Kyle, turned their horses back the way they had come. Davey led the way and Kyle followed closely behind Wes, his handgun still drawn. Looking at the steepness of the ascent, Wes hoped that Ned would be as sure-footed on the slope as he was on the flat. Summing up the two gang members Wes surmised that Davey was the more senior, definitely the more intelligent, while Kyle was a little unbalanced; his whole demeanour smacked of locoweed. He was high on something, the kind to shoot just for the excitement of squeezing the trigger.

Ned was a good, strong quarter horse, not bred for climbing mountains, but sturdy and reliable. Even with all the extra load of Alice and her baggage he negotiated the twisty and narrow track safely, which wound its way up through the vertical outcrops and treacherous scree. They passed the fabled two trees, which were very much bigger than they appeared from the distance of the lower slope, and soon came to a surprisingly large open area where ice and snow had once carved out a hollow, leaving a rainwater pond in the very centre. The surrounding ground, at once rocky and soft with centuries of ground-down rockdust, rocky shards and wind-blown sand was now home to three tent-like structures of canvas and tarpaulins. A rough part-timber, part-tarp shack was the only solid-looking dwelling. At the back of the hollow a fire blazed next to a stack of pine lumber cut from the woods below and hauled up to the fuel store. A group of hobbled horses stared at the new arrivals. A stunted pine, probably grown from the seed of a wind-blown cone many years ago, flourished in the shelter of the hollow, but would never reach much of a height in such poor soil. It provided the only substantial vegetation, while tenacious mountain plants dotted cracks in the rock-face with points of green and the occasional white or yellow flower. Moss and lichens were more abundant than grass as a covering for the thin soil.

Three men were sitting or lying close to the fire, the large platform of wooden planks raised just enough to keep them off the cold ground and provide a good, level surface. Chairs and large cushions, probably stuffed with hay and straw, gave the scene a touch of unlikely comfort for a bandit hideout. An elaborate metal structure straddled the fire and the smell of searing beef wafted on the swirls of air. It was an incongruously homely scene.

One of the lounging gang leapt to his feet as soon as the new party entered the hollow. He drew his gun and approached Davey.

'What's doing, Davey?'

'Found this bounty hunter down in the valley, making his way to the track. And guess who he's got on board.'

'I'm no bounty hun—' Wes began, but he was quickly halted.

'Shut yer mouth, son,' ordered the new man, his gun pointing at Wes immediately.

A voice called over from by the fire. 'What've we got, boys?'

Wes recognized the speaker instantly and took no notice of the order to keep his mouth closed. 'Doyle! It's me, Wesley Vernon, your old buddy.'

'Wesley Vernon? Wes? What in hell are you doin' here? It's all right, boys; he's no bounty hunter. You're not a lawman now, are you, Wes?'

'Hell no. I've come to join up.'

Casey and the other man got up off the platform and came over to the group. Everyone was dismounted and introductions took place. In his immediate satisfaction of achieving his first goal, that of finding Doyle Casey, Wes had momentarily set aside the mystery of Alice. But once he and she were accepted as non-threatening visitors he started to wonder why she was recognized by Kyle, and apparently known to the outlaws.

Two more slabs of steak were thrown onto the metal griddle, mugs of beer were poured from a barrel, whiskey was served in small glasses and the gathering was more like a homecoming.

'So, Wes, my old school mate, what really brings you to these parts? And who told you how to find me?'

Wes had to be careful. The free flow of liquor, the smell of sizzling steak, the relief of not being killed out-of-hand, the prospect of accomplishing his mission, could all lead to a careless word that might raise suspicion. Worst of all, he could see Doyle was a shrewd and cunning fox who was on his guard constantly. The years

87

had not been kind to his childhood friend. His cheeks were drawn in, his skin rather sallow and stubble did nothing to improve his appearance. Only his piercing blue eyes were unchanged, still giving the uncanny feeling of seeing right into your very core. Wes began his prepared story.

'I've been working as a mine engineer. I'm an explosives man. I know just where and how to lay charges to blow rock faces safely to kingdom come, and small charges down a shaft to open difficult seams. I'd heard talk that people who used to know you thought you'd become an outlaw, so when mine work began to dry up, I thought you might be able to use me and my skills. Bank walls, vaults and safes are a lot easier to blow than controlled explosions in a mineshaft.'

'You're a sly one, Wes. Always thought you were going to be some big successful businessman. Remember when we were playing Civil War battles and how you negotiated all those wooden soldiers from that old miser in the local store? You wheedled him down to half price if we bought the whole lot. I'll never forget that. It was a lesson in life for me, that was. What happened to that side of you?'

Wes eased into the conversation and made no silly mistakes. The rest of the gang listened, finding out stuff they'd never heard about their leader's childhood. The conversation was light and relaxed. But then Doyle turned to Alice.

'Well, well, here's our pretty little puma with claws to match. Have you seen Berney's face, Alice? Look what you done to him. Go on Berney; show her. Scottie here said he should've shot you, you little bitch. Berney was too soft. But now that you've turned up, you might want to put things right by him.'

Alice said nothing but she turned her head away. Wes could only guess at what must have taken place at the hold-up. Perhaps that's why they left her for dead.

Casey rolled himself a smoke, and while he did so nobody spoke. Without making it obvious, Wes looked round at the gang. Doyle Casey, very much in charge; Davey, probably his right hand man; and three drifters: adrenaline Kyle with the silly laugh, Berney with the nail-gashed face, and Scottie, who hadn't yet said a single word. Wes wished he'd left Alice in Avondale; what he had now found out made her a liability rather than an asset. As it turned out, he didn't need her to masquerade as his wife, and now it seemed he might have to protect her from the masculine desires of the bandits. Having rolled his smoke and puffed out a few times, Casey sprang to his feet.

'Wes, come with me. There's someone I'd like you to meet. It's gonna be a surprise. You'd never guess.'

Wes got to his feet and Casey led the way across to the rough wooden and tarp construction. In his mind Wes was thinking he knew whom it would be: the business-man with a bank in Boston or New York, taken hostage at the hold-up. The conjunction of Boston, bank and man going to Sweetspring added up to only one possible person. What a coincidence! He wondered what the gang planned to do with the man. It might solve a problem for Wes if he was killed. The east coast was much too far away to plan a bank raid; there must be some other idea in Casey's mind. Ransom, perhaps? As they reached the shack, Casey pushed open the door.

'Honey, someone to see you.'

It was not quite dark inside the dwelling, if it could be called that. Wes could see a table, a couple of chairs and the main piece of furniture, which was a large bed piled with covers against the bitter cold of the night air. The covers stirred and a head emerged.

Casey prodded the figure under the stack of blankets. 'She hasn't been feeling too good. Having a rest, aren't you, honey? Look who's here: our old friend, Wes.' He turned to Wesley. 'You remember Aimee? Of course you do. She's still as beautiful as ever, ain't she?'

The figure sat up in bed, decidedly dishevelled, rubbing her eyes. 'Wesley Vernon? You gotta be kidding. Really, it's Wes?' She flopped back semi-comatose.

Casey pushed Wes back out through the door and they left Aimee to her slumbers. 'You didn't expect that, did you?'

'No, I sure did not,' Wes agreed.

At once it was clear why Casey was reluctant to attack the interests of the Vangraf Express Company. It was something Wes had guessed at but never really thought could be so. Why in hell would Aimee Vangraf, with her prospects of one day inheriting a huge fortune, and right now being able to live a life of easy luxury, want to shack up with a no-good, ridge-riding, pock-faced, scruffy sonofabitch like Doyle Casey? For all his fond memories of a fun-packed childhood and prank-filled youth with his best friend Doyle, Wes could now see his former inseparable buddy for what he was, and he didn't like it one little bit. Surely Aimee wasn't here of her own free will. Was she drugged? Then the idea occurred to Wes that Doyle was holding Aimee to ensure Vangraf took no action against him in a mutual standoff. So many possibilities. Wes realized he hadn't just caught up with his old friend; he'd walked into the lair of a vicious mountain lion.

'Well, now you know everything about me,' Casey said, in a rather proud way. 'This place is only a rough hideout, you understand. We've got a ranch further north of here where I keep all my cattle and horses, a fully-fledged legitimate business. We just hole up here during the robbing season.' He laughed. 'It's an easy life. All the proceeds go into the cattle, nobody can ever pin anything on me. I'm a big noise in the local cattle association up north, you know.'

Like all men who live on the edge of legality, and are proud to, Doyle Casey was full of his self-importance and self-adoration, besotted with the idea that he was really an honest dealer in cattle and horses, a very successful entrepreneur, when in fact he was nothing more than the dregs of humanity, the scum that lives off the efforts of honest men, that takes instead of makes, that thieves instead of grafts, that impoverishes communities instead of enriching them. Wes had to overcome his distaste for what his one-time friend had become. People can change over time; Doyle Casey certainly had. But Wesley's priority, beyond concealing his true intention, was to protect Alice whom he thought was now at great risk of violation.

'So how did you hook up with Alice?' Doyle asked.

'Just passing the overturned coach? I thought we'd left only dead bodies behind.'

'Yes,' Wes replied, thinking fast. 'That's exactly it. You know she tried to fool me and steal my horse? Clever bitch.'

'Clever bitch, indeed. We thought she was dead and done for. She clambered onto the coach after gouging Davey, he fired a shot at her, and she screamed and fell through the doorway. We left her for dead.'

'Have you got a spare bed for us?'

'Us?' queried Casey. 'You and Alice? Davey might have something to say about that.'

'I know. I know. I guess he should get first shout.'

'He should,' Casey agreed. 'But look, you're an old friend, and actually I'm rather pleased to see my old buddy. So you get first go with her, Davey can wait his turn. One of the tents is almost free. We've got another guest right now, but I can move him out and into the brushwood shelter. He needs softening up; not yet co-operative enough.'

'Who is he?'

'Won't tell us his name, or anything else, but I could see he was a rich bastard: fine clothes, gold rings, smooth skin and hands. Someone will pay to get him back.'

Wes suddenly had an idea. 'Look, say you leave him in the tent with me and Alice. Let me pump him carefully for information. He might be more willing to speak to me, especially if you introduce us as two more hostages.'

'Say, that's a mighty shrewd idea, Wes. See, I always knew you were the smart one.'

The evening continued round the fire with stories

that got more outrageous and exaggerated as the day-light went to dusk, then to dusky black. On a mountaintop it never quite reaches the same intensity of pitch black that you get in the valleys; there's always some lightness in the visible sky from the myriad stars. When it was time to turn in, Alice had the good sense not to comment when Casey told her that she'd be shacking up with Wes and to look after him real good. Casey took them over to the tent. He pulled the flap aside and shoved them in.

'Mr Moneybags Businessman! Look, I've brought another two to keep you company,' he laughed convincingly and shoved them in, making Alice stumble forward. The candle that Casey had supplied kindly for Wes threw a dim orange glow into the tent. Wes saw at once why the hostage had made no reply: he was bound, gagged and lying on a makeshift mattress with insufficient covers. Wes took pity on him: this was no way to treat a hostage if Casey wanted him to talk, but it did give Wes an immediate opportunity for friendliness. He gave the candle to Alice, then, taking a few covers that were stacked up on three other bedrolls in the tent, Wes put them over the man. Then he freed the gag, but didn't untie his hands or legs: he didn't want to give away all his inducements in one go. The man spat out bits of the ragged gag that he'd chewed off. Wes put the man's water flask to his mouth and he drank greedily. He'd obviously been left like this for quite a while to make him more compliant.

'We're all in this together, mister,' Wes began. He turned to Alice. 'Is this the man who was in the

93

stagecoach with you?'

Alice held the candle nearer the man's face. 'Yes. It's him.'

'Untie me,' the man pleaded.

'Not yet. Not until I'm sure I can trust you. Play your cards right and we'll all get out of this with our lives. A false move and they'll kill all three of us. You don't mess with Doyle Casey.'

It wasn't as cold in the tent as Wesley had feared. It was a good quality tarp and probably double layered against the mountain air. Wes took the candle back and pointed to the bed furthest from the hostage. He told Alice to get under the covers and get some sleep.

She hesitated. 'Do you mean I've got to sleep in here with you two?' she said rather stupidly, since it was perfectly clear.

'Or with Davey,' Wes offered. 'I can always call Casey back.'

Alice immediately put her hand on Wes's arm. 'No.'

'Well, I said you should be my wife, didn't I? Now hush up and sort yourself out, or I'll demand my rights!'

Nothing more was heard from Alice except the rustling of the covers as she disappeared beneath a pile of furs and blankets.

Wes slipped into the bedroll next to the hostage. 'I'm your only hope to a safe passage out of this fix, mister, so trust me if you want to live, otherwise you're dead meat. Now, tell me your name and where you were headed.'

'I guess I don't have a choice. I hope you're a man of your word.'

'Whatever else I am, you can count on my word,

mister. I've never broken it yet.'

The man heaved a resigned sigh. 'My name's Emile. My father's an important businessman back east. I run a chain of banks, the largest one is in Boston. The bank would pay a significant ransom but I don't want these scum to know that.'

'I think they already do; they've guessed you're a money ticket. You've dressed up too much. Bad mistake out west, unless you've got good protection. Where were you headed?'

'Coldbush.'

'What was your business in Coldbush? Not the sort of place for big business.'

'You don't need to know about that.'

'Suit yourself.' Wes left the conversation with that and pretended to settle down. With the information that Alice had given him earlier, he then said, 'I'd heard you were going to Sweetspring.'

'Sweetspring!' the man repeated. 'Where did you hear that?'

Wes had been keeping this up his sleeve for a while, now it was time to roll the dice and gamble.

'If you can keep it quiet I'll tell you. I came out looking for you.'

'For me?'

'Yes, Emile. Henry Mancini sent me to find you. You are Emile Laroche?'

'Yes. Henry sent you? Why?'

'I don't know. I was just told to look out for Emile Laroche at Coldbush. So when I came across the remnants of a holdup and discovered someone was missing,

I put two and two together.'

As an explanation the entire story was full of holes, but people are often willing to believe what they hear, especially if it's what they want to hear, rather than what logic tells them can or can't be true.

'Extraordinary!' Laroche exclaimed. 'That's just like Mancini. Looking after his own interests. You see, I'm to marry his daughter Madeleine; it's part of a business deal from which he gains a share in my banking operation. What an extraordinary fellow Mancini is! I swear he'll be governor one day. Now I really can sleep in peace, thanks to you.'

Wes had gambled and won the bet, but it made him far from happy. In fact, it plunged him into the depth of despair. He now knew for certain what he suspected when Alice had described her fellow passengers. A most extraordinary coincidence. Or was it? Wes knew very well this man was on his way to Sweetspring and he had good reason to stop him. Was he playing a dangerous game, even more dangerous than the apparent mission of hunting down Doyle Casey? Or was it just incredible good luck that had delivered this man into his mercy . . . Mercy? Wes was gripped by an almost overwhelming desire to strangle this man in the night. How easy it would be to strangle him. What would be the consequences? Wes loosened his neckerchief. How easy to do it right now, and face the consequences later. Consequences. Throw the stone into the pool and hope the ripples don't spread too far.

10

Waking in the hour or two after midnight, Wes tossed and turned. Alice was sound asleep; he could hear her regular breathing under the covers. Emile Laroche was lying on his side, facing away from Wes and also asleep, but snoring gently. Maybe what Wes had said to him had enabled him to drop into a deep sleep; perhaps he hadn't slept much the night before in captivity fearing for his life. If he had known what Wes was turning over in his mind he would still be equally fearful. But whatever Wes was, or whatever opportunity was presenting itself to him, Wes was not a cold-blooded murderer, however much he stood to gain from such an act.

Morning came in due course. Wes had not slept enough, but he had formulated a plan. He had decided that his priority was still Doyle Casey. As for Alice and Emile, they were sideshows. When Wes poked his head outside the tent, he could see Berney acting as cook. The fire was being stoked up and water was boiling for coffee. Wes decided to be generous. He wandered over to Berney.

'Could you use some more supplies?'

'We can always use more supplies,' Berney confirmed. 'We're a greedy band!'

'Well, I've got some flour and beans you can have.' Wes went to his saddle-bags and removed the items.

Casey emerged from his wooden shack. 'You've come well-prepared,' he said, seeing the flour and beans.

'I figured if I wanted to join you I ought to make a contribution.' He gave the supplies to Berney and then walked back to Casey, who was still doing up the buttons on his shirt. 'I brought something else useful as well.'

He led Doyle over to his saddlebags stacked in the shelter and withdrew a stick of dynamite. 'And I know how to use it. I thought you might want to try blowing out a bank wall. Saves the risk of a daylight holdup.'

Casey looked at the stick of explosive in Wes's hand. 'Very timely. I've got my eye on a bank in Courtney Crossing, a busy and expanding town about forty miles south of here. Do you know it? We could try it down there. You sure you know what you're doing?'

Wes nodded. The seed was sown. All he had to do was go along with Casey's plan and look for his opportunity.

'Another thing you might like to know. Your hostage spilled the beans last night. He owns a banking concern back east and I know exactly how we can get them to pay. They'll pay big money.'

Casey smiled and clapped Wes on the back. 'Do you know, Wes, if I didn't know you were an old friend, I'd think you were a clever plant, something like a Texas ranger or federal marshal inveigled into my band to trip me up and turn me in.'

Wes Vernon and Doyle Casey, childhood buddies, now grown men, arms round each other's shoulders, both laughed; but not for the same reason.

Over a breakfast of warmed-up stew, Wes learnt that Berney was the gang's chuck wagon chief and Scottie was the scout – they'd originally called him Scouty but he said Scottie sounded better. Casey did all the planning, of course. Davey was the best stake-out man, according to Casey: he could mix with any crowd or observe any bank without being noticed by anyone, but now that he had huge red welts down his left cheek he was literally a marked man and much too distinctive. Kyle was a loose cannon, much too unstable to take over from Davey, and so it was something of a surprise when Casey suggested to Wes that he might like to take a look at the bank in Courtney as the gang's new stakeout ghost. Wes realized this would be his first test of usefulness to the gang.

Casey took Wes aside after breakfast. 'I've been worried that some of the gang may have been seen on some of the raids. There are a dozen reward dodgers for us posted all over the county, most with drawings that look like any saddletramp who's fallen on hard times. They're the imaginings of an amateur artist rather than eyewitness descriptions. But nobody has seen you round these parts, so you can act natural, like a traveller looking for work. You and Scottie can go together.'

'To make sure Scottie keeps an eye on me.'

'Yeah,' Casey agreed, then smiled. 'Only joshing, Wes.

Four eyes are better than two. Scottie can keep a lookout while you take a look at the bank walls for thickness. See if your firesticks can blow a hole . . .'

'My dynamite could blow a whole block to kingdom come, don't you worry about that. The trick is to do only as much damage as is needed. Anyways, I know what information I need. When do we go?'

'You and Scottie ride off before dawn tomorrow. Shack up in the town overnight and come back the day after with the detail. Scottie will sketch a map of the streets round the bank and the routes in and out of the town. He's very thorough, that's his job. Make sure you're good at yours.'

Most of the day was spent lazing around the hollow. There was nothing much to do. Berney made a foray into Avondale to get some supplies. Kyle kept lookout by Two Trees. Doyle and Davey were in conference together. Aimee and Alice had discovered each other and were trading stories. Wes took the opportunity to talk to Emile about his business interests. He deliberately kept his voice low in the tent and talked earnestly with the hostage, whose hands and legs were still bound.

'Listen to me, Emile. Your life is in danger. You're not worth much to the gang and when they tire of pursuing a reward with Boston, which is too far away to do business with, they'll pitch you over the edge of a ravine. Now, I'm going to give your legs a bit of freedom if you give your word that you'll keep quiet about the things I'm going to tell you.'

Laroche gave his word and Wes untied the leg shackles. Wes then proceeded to paint a picture of corruption in Sweetspring and sow seeds of doubt in Emile's mind about what he might be getting himself into if he went into partnership with Mancini. Knowing Henry Mancini very well, Wes was able to present a very convincing portrait to Laroche with more than enough detail to be utterly believable. Having sketched out Mancini's very dubious business empire and his political aspirations Wes then delivered the hammer blow.

'You've met his daughter, Madeleine?'

'Yes of course,' Laroche confirmed. 'I knew her while she was studying in Boston. That's how we met.'

'But you must know she isn't in love with you. She has a regular fellow in Sweetspring. I've seen them together many times. They look to be very much in love with each other.'

Laroche laughed quietly. 'She's been promised to me, don't you worry about that. Mancini won't go back on his word. He needs my backing to get him into the highest political office in the state.'

Wes scrutinized Laroche's features. Was he really the kind of man Maddy would want to be seen with? Unfortunately, the answer to that was probably yes. He was in his early thirties with a good head of very black hair, not so well groomed just now, but well cut. His features were attractively symmetrical, his eyes were a soft grey colour and the few smile lines in the corner of his eyes suggested a man who could enjoy a joke. His skin had the smoothness belying any suggestion of a hard life. This man was clearly wealthy and used to a very comfortable life.

It puzzled Wes why Laroche would want to expand

101

his business into the west. Could there really be so much opportunity in these vast semi-desert wastes, except for cattle or sinking thousands of dollars into mineral speculation? One thing was fairly sure: Maddy wasn't in love with him. She couldn't possibly have been so shallow as to be swayed by wealth. Maddy was in love with himself, Wes, wasn't she? But he couldn't help looking at Laroche and comparing himself unfavourably with the rich, successful, suave person sitting in front of him. Just suppose Maddy had really taken a liking to Laroche. How would she feel seeing him again? It was something Wes felt he had to prevent at all costs. He replaced the shackles on Laroche's legs and unbound his hands.

'Get the circulation going while I tell you what I'm going to do for you.'

Laroche rubbed his wrists, which were deeply marked with an impression of the rough fibre rope. He shook his hands and stretched his fingers. Wes noticed they were long and slender with the nails well trimmed. Only the stubble was disguising Emile's attention to personal grooming.

Wes continued. 'I'm going to get you out of here, on one condition. It will be highly dangerous for myself to get you away, but while my stock of goodwill is still high I think I can get away with it.'

'What's the condition?' Laroche wondered.

'You go straight back to Boston and forget all about Sweetspring.'

Laroche's eyes narrowed, his brow furrowed with a deep frown and his head turned slightly sideways.

'What's your game? What do you gain in this?'

It was a good question and a difficult one to answer. Wes was caught on the hop; he hadn't thought that one through properly.

'You're going to give me a thousand dollar reward when I'm done here and show up in Boston.'

'Money. It's always money. And if I refuse?'

'Do so and look over your shoulder for the rest of your life.'

It was a menacing threat delivered uncharacteristically with venomous intent. Wes surprised himself, and realized that an unhealthy jealousy had pushed him to the edge of restraint. This very worthy competitor had to be removed, but Wes would not stoop to anything underhand; above all he remained true to his conviction that wrongs must be righted by the law and only by the law. But in affairs of the heart the law counted for nothing and frequently made men act irrationally and unlawfully. A man without Wes's moral fortitude would have simply planned for Laroche to escape and shot him in the back during the attempt.

'Tonight, I'll untie you and free you. You will have to go on foot and get as far away as you can by the light of the stars. Don't go to Avondale; that's the first place they'll look for you. I'll give you a packet of cold pork and biscuits. Stay well away from any roads for a couple of days. Then head east and get a ride with any passing wagon. You must go east, go back to Boston; they're bound to think you're still heading for Sweetspring.'

Although Wes, of course, wanted Laroche to head east and go back where he came from, he was also right in his belief that this was Laroche's best chance of escape. Wes could see there was no hope of Casey negotiating a reward with a bank a couple of thousand miles away. Laroche would be killed sooner or later. Knowing this, Wes felt he would be complicit in the murder if he didn't try to do something to prevent it. How he wished he could ignore his moral compass.

For the rest of the day, Wes mooched about, talking to Alice, eating, drinking and talking with the gang members. He kept searching his conscience to reassure himself he was going to be doing the right thing. Secretly he could not get rid of the idea that what he really wanted was for Emile Laroche to disappear and never be seen again. However, the more important matter was to be ready to leave at dawn with Scottie and ride to Courtney Crossing.

That night, when Wes turned in, he dared to say a silent prayer that nothing would stand between him and Maddy, and nothing would frustrate his self-appointed mission to bring Doyle Casey to justice. A tall order: he would need God on his side every step of the way. When he was satisfied the camp was totally quiet, Wes shook Emile Laroche gently.

'It's time, buddy.'

He cut the wrist rope, released the leg shackles, handed over the packet of food and saw Laroche safely out of the tent. Clouds passed slowly across the sky, briefly obliterating the sliver of moon, but the stars sparkled and the hollow was illuminated in a ghostly, ethereal light. A thin blanket of mist hung over the pond, adding to the secretive atmosphere of escape and deception. It was completely quiet: not even the hoot of an owl or the bark of a dog fox disturbed the silence. Laroche, at first hesitant, turned and shook Wes by the hand, said thank you and picked his way carefully and noiselessly towards the gap. Wes watched him all the way across the hollow until he disappeared down the track. He closed the tent flap, sighed and lay down on his bed.

Alice stirred. 'Wesley, I'm cold. Lie next to me.'

'It wouldn't be proper,' he said, shocked.

'But it would be nice. I want some warmth. You're fully clothed aren't you?'

'Yes, I am.'

'Well then?'

There was no point in having an argument. It wasn't as if he was going to . . . to . . . well, *do* anything. So he relented and got under the covers with Alice.

'Lie on you side,' he demanded. 'No. Facing the other way. Now you can wriggle back a bit.' Dutifully he let her reverse into him and they lay there together, completely innocently, although Wes wasn't so sure about Alice.

The nervous energy of seeing Laroche safely on his way had taken its toll. Wes's thoughts went to Maddy, his sweetheart in Sweetspring. He mouthed a word of reassurance silently to Maddy about lying so close to Alice. It was nothing immoral and nothing he would be ashamed of; Maddy need not give it a moment's thought. At least he hoped she would never need to hear about it, and promptly he fell fast asleep.

11

It seemed as if he had only just gone to sleep when Wes woke with a start. He could hear movement outside the tent. Immediately he thought of Laroche. Had he come back? What for? Why hadn't he made good his escape? Now, not only had he signed his own death warrant, he had jeopardized Wes's good relationship with the gang and very probably ruined all his plans. He could hear the horses stomping. Surely Laroche hadn't come back to steal a horse!

Hastily, Wes eased himself out of the covers, trying not to disturb Alice, who was still attached to him in a foetal position. He grabbed his gun-belt, fumbled with the buckle, drew the Colt and stuck his head outside the tent. It was less dark than before. In fact, the sky was beginning to lighten away to the east. In a moment Wes saw Scottie untying his horse and loading up his saddlebags. Of course: everything fell into place. It was time for him and Scottie to set out for Courtney Crossing. Hours had passed, not minutes. Wes gathered his saddlebags from inside the tent and came out to greet Scottie.

'All set?'

'Ready to go,' Scottie replied.

Forty or so miles is not a huge distance to travel on a horse but, there being no hurry, the two bandits – for that is what they were – took their time. Wes knew he would have to go through with blasting the bank if he was to retain his credibility with Casey. Not only that, he would have to do a good job to be accepted. They planned to arrive in Courtney Crossing mid-afternoon when activity at the bank would be picking up with the daily deposits from traders. Casey had also selected now as a good time because springtime cattle sales had increased the flow of cash into the town. Nervous ranchers would deposit their earnings in the bank, being the only safe place to keep large sums – at least under normal circumstances. Courtney Crossing was about to discover that these were not normal circumstances.

Scottie drew his maps and travelled carefully through the ins and outs of the town to be thoroughly familiar with how he would lead the gang in and away. Wes made a careful study of the outside walls of the bank, and spending just a few minutes inside enabled him to observe the layout and locate the most likely position of the safe: neatly tucked away in the back room and conveniently placed against an exterior wall. A common mistake.

They lodged overnight in a cheap boarding house on the outskirts of the town, somewhere they could merge unnoticeably into the faded wallpaper and creaking beds. They ate a tough steak and drank stale beer. Scottie settled down for the night in the company of a tawdry, powdered lady of questionable virtue, but Wes claimed he had to make some important calculations and avoided an awkward encounter. Even so, it didn't prevent him being woken in the night by a female in the flimsiest of night attire to see if he needed anything. He said he was perfectly fine, thank you, and what he needed most was a good night's sleep. She said it would only cost a couple of dollars for her to stay for the rest of the night. He declined again, and the price eventually dropped to fifty cents; she was desperate for some company.

'Look, miss,' Wes said politely, although he knew she was twice the age of any miss he had ever met. 'Come back in the morning and I'll give you a dollar, but leave me in peace right now.'

'A dollar,' she whispered, and slid into the bed. 'You don't want to waste that dollar, do you?'

For the second time in as many days, Wes mouthed a silent prayer. *Don't you worry, Maddy, she isn't going to get anything from me other than the coin!*

Wes was up good and early, but Scottie didn't put in an appearance until long gone sun-up. He came down the stairs doing up his trousers and trying to hold onto his gun-belt at the same time, but he couldn't do the two things together, so the gun-belt and the trousers both descended and tripped him up on the last tread of the stair.

'God damn it, ' he screamed, clambering to his feet.

Lukewarm coffee, cold bacon, undercooked beans and a hunk of day-old sourdough did nothing to restore his good humour. They were both glad to emerge into daylight, satisfied to see their horses and not to have been robbed in the night. Ironically, no traveller was entirely safe in a place like that.

Later that day, Casey was pleased to see them back at the hollow. But the news that the Bostonian hostage had escaped in the night was a shock. Wes's nerves tightened when Casey said he'd already punished the culprit.

'Little bitch cut his rope and somehow removed the shackles.' Casey looked directly at Wes. 'Must've done it after you left with Scottie.'

'Did she admit it?' Wes queried, his heart in his mouth.

'Not exactly.'

'But?'

Casey smirked. 'She wouldn't say how she did it. Two gentle smacks were enough.'

Wes blinked and jerked his head away, as if he was now receiving the blows that Alice must have endured. He steeled himself for what he knew was a horrible lie. 'I knew there was something between them. They didn't just meet on the coach by chance. She already knew Laroche. Maybe he's gone for help?'

'Well, maybe. I think he's more likely to save his own skin. He had no spine in him. Alice will tell us more when she can talk again!'

That was the end of the matter. Everyone dispersed. Wes and Scottie unloaded their horses. With terrible misgivings, Wes approached the tent. What would he find? At once he saw Alice, her back to the world, lying on her bed. He approached her slowly.

'Alice. Alice, what did he do?'

She didn't move. She was sobbing. Gently, Wes took her shoulder and eased her round slowly. Her eyes were puffy from the crying, but one was swollen nastily, almost closed, and the surrounding area very red. She shook her head slowly and Wes noticed the other side of her face was twice its normal size, her lips were bloated, her mouth horribly distorted and the red welt of the injury was already turning blue as the bruising took hold. Wes ran his hand over her forehead to smooth away the damp hair.

'You suffered this for me?' were the only words he could bring himself to utter before returning Alice to her original position. Feebly, he stroked her shoulder before turning away with a sickness in the pit of his stomach. A vengeful fire began to burn inside. Any man who can do that kind of thing to a woman forfeits the right to be called a man. He left the tent to join the discussion about the raid.

It was agreed that the next day was to be a day of rest and preparation: a day to clean guns, polish and check horse harness, and make sure other equipment was clean and serviceable. The raid would be in two days' time. It was decided that Wes would ride into Courtney on his own before sun-up and place the charges. The rest of the gang would ride in after midday when the townsfolk would be at dinner and fewer people would be roaming the streets. Wes was secretly nervous: he knew his trade, his craft, but he was mindful that, while he wanted to open up a hole in the bank and blow the

110

safe, he didn't want any innocent civilians to be caught up in the explosions or killed by the flying debris. These weren't his only concerns. There was also the problem of Alice. He felt a new kind of responsibility towards her. What could he do about that? It wouldn't be safe to leave her with the gang. And there was one other person he hadn't yet had the chance to talk to, but it was imperative he explained what he was trying to do. Tomorrow would be more than just a preparation of equipment; Wes had people to prepare as well.

On the following day there was a calm about the camp. Everyone was engaged in their own world of activity. Everyone except Kyle, who had been sent off on an errand of some sort. Wes guessed it was always like this. There was never any guarantee that everyone would return from a raid, or that if they did they wouldn't be nursing a potentially fatal wound from some lucky shot or a chance encounter with a particularly coura-geous sharp-shooting deputy. Each was in their own thoughts about what the raid might mean for them.

During the quiet time after the midday meal, when everyone was resting, Wes took the opportunity to talk to Aimee. He said he wanted to talk to her privately. She took him into the shack. Out of Casey's earshot, he asked Aimee how she was doing, how had her life turned out and whether she remember their childhood days when he and Doyle had both been chasing her.

'Of course I do. You always hung back, Wes, as if you knew Doyle was going to be the one who would catch my eye.'

'He did, didn't he? I always knew it. Are you happy?'

111

'Happy? What's that? I never think about being happy, but I wish Doyle would give up this way of life. We've got a good ranch up north, beef cattle, fine horses, all we could need, men to run the place, and more cash than we could ever use, but I can't persuade him to give this up. He lives on the excitement. If this bank raid comes off tomorrow, we'll have another haul of cash and stuff, but we don't need it. We've got everything we need, except children. I want children; I want to raise a family. Doyle says yes but not yet.'

'Suppose I could change his mind? Would you want me to?'

Aimee gave Wes a sideways glance. 'How would you do that?'

'Never mind. Would you trust me?'

'Maybe.'

'No, I need better assurance than that. I'm confident I can get him to see reason and give up this useless existence. But I need your absolute trust, and absolute secrecy about what I'm going to tell you.'

Just then the door burst open and Doyle strode into the room. He slapped Aimee hard round the face. Wes stood up but Doyle drew his six-gun and pressed the barrel into Wes's chest, forcing him back into the chair.

'Snake. Wesley Vernon, you've come here to try and steal my girl, haven't you? Never quite accepted that Aimee chose me instead of you, is that it?'

Wesley's hands were half up in the air in a sign of resignation. He suddenly feared for his life, but couldn't hold back on the truth. 'No, Doyle. Not Aimee. It's you I've come for.'

'And you think I didn't know? You think I'm so stupid that you're looking up a friend for old times' sake? Wise up, Wesley. Do you think I didn't recognize you at the raid on Gudrun's mine? I even guessed you might have recognized me, and it might be you who followed us after shooting that bank clerk and doing the bank in Sweetspring. I didn't know you worked at the mine, or that you lived in Sweetspring, but I knew you as soon as I saw you. I could have killed you when you were tracking us, but when I recognized you again in my gunsight, I thought a shot in the leg would warn you off. I guess that was my mistake. I spared you for old times' sake. I never expected you to turn up here.'

'So what now?' Wes asked. 'A shot to finish me off?'

'Not yet. What were you talking to Aimee about?'

Wes wondered if Aimee would back him up or make matters worse. He had to take a chance. 'Nothing important, just how life had been treating her and whether she was happy now.'

Doyle looked at Aimee. 'Is that so?'

Wes held his breath. Aimee looked at him, her face colouring up with the blow. 'Yes,' she said to Doyle. 'That was all. I promise.'

Doyle turned back to Wes. 'Nothing changes with our plans. You set your charges tomorrow. Do it properly. Foul up and Alice gets shot, do you understand? You're such an upright fellow, Wesley. I figure that if you think someone else will suffer for your mistakes you'll be a good deal more careful. It would be such a pity if Alice had to take the bullet for you. Have you slept with her yet?'

Wes was caught. Yes he had and no he hadn't – not in the sense that Casey meant. 'What does it matter?'

'Perhaps you should tonight.' Casey cajoled. 'Just don't try anything funny. Run off and Alice gets it. Clear?'

'I'm not going anywhere,' Wes asserted. 'You gave me a job to do tomorrow and I intend to do it.'

That night, Wes rearranged the bedding. Alice slept in her underclothes to keep warm. Wes slept fully clothed, gun-belt aside, as did all the bandits, not wanting to be caught by a posse ill prepared and only in their longjohns. He slid under the pile of warm blankets, now spread over the width of two mattresses. Alice had her back to him. Carefully he eased himself next to her, leant over and kissed her very lightly on the cheek.

'Thank you,' he said softly, close to her ear. 'I won't forget what you've done for me.'

The camp stirred before sunrise. Casey was up to see that Wes was ready to go off early. They exchanged a few words before Wes set off down the track, Ned picking his way carefully across the dew-slippery stones. Emerging from the hollow and passing the two gaunt skeletons of the eponymous pines, the track was easy enough to see, and Ned, with his light-enhancing animal eyes, had no difficulty in an alternate diagonal descent and getting safely to the foot of the almost sheer slope. Wes felt this was a weakness in the plan. He should have set off last night if he was to plant the charges before the town came to life. Ned couldn't gallop for forty miles; no horse would do that. So he

114

couldn't see how he would be in Courtney before the middle of the morning. It suddenly occurred to him that Casey might have set him up. Had Kyle been sent to town the day before for just such a purpose? There was no reason for Wes to change his own plan. He was happy to let things take their own course.

As it happened it was still fairly early in the day when Wes reached the outskirts of Courtney Crossing. At the town limits a signboard proclaimed a God-fearing town of major commercial opportunity that had no truck with outlaws or unlawful traders, and warned those engaged in such activities to move on. Wes smiled as he noticed two splintering gunshot holes each through the letter 'o' in Courtney and Crossing. Not everyone followed the town council's wishes!

Wes headed straight for the sheriff's office and hitched Ned to the rail. The window blinds were still half down; maybe the sheriff hadn't roused himself yet. In fact, he was standing at the gun rack checking the row of Winchesters with a deputy as Wes opened the door. The sheriff wheeled round.

'Good morning, Sheriff,' Wes began brightly. 'I've got some information that might be of interest to you.'

12

Wes pulled up a chair. The sheriff sat at his desk. The deputy took over checking each Winchester in turn. The sheriff picked up a mug and drank some coffee. It was cold and he spat it back into the mug.

'Jerry! More coffee.'

Wes leant forward in his chair. 'My name's Wesley Vernon. I'm a mine engineer from Sweetspring.'

'Would you like some coffee, Mr Vernon?'

'Matter of fact, I would.'

The sheriff made it clear he wasn't ready to listen until he had some fresh coffee in front of him. He rapped his fingers on the desk, possibly to some tune in his mind, possibly just a random thing. Wes became impatient; he had a lot to do before the gang came into town.

Waiting a full four minutes for the coffee to brew before he was allowed to begin, it took no more than a quarter of an hour to secure the sheriff's understanding and co-operation. Wes left the sheriff's office both pleased and despondent. If everything went to plan his mission would be accomplished. But despondency warned him that no bank raid ever went to plan. Something always happened to foul it up.

Under the watchful eye of Jerry, the sheriff's deputy, and with the full understanding of the amazed bank manager, Wes placed a sufficient quantity of dynamite to blow a hole in the wall without reducing the bank to rubble. It was probable that it would not be enough, but the safety of the town's inhabitants was uppermost in the sheriff's consent. The sheriff allowed Wes to do what he had to, as a tempting reward was promised. The prize for Doyle Casey's gang was substantial, according to all the dodgers, and there were two pinned up in Courtney. The gang had become a serious threat to the county's prosperity. The sheriff could see his own name up in lights, feted by the whole county for bringing Casey to justice. Maybe it would even put him in the running for an important elected post; town mayor would be a first step.

It required a deal of the sheriff's ingenuity to post enough deputies to keep people away from the bank without arousing the townsfolk's curiosity. When the gang rode into town, an entire posse of newly sworn deputies would be at the ready. Wes retired to the place previously agreed with Scottie, from which he would be able to see the gang approaching and ignite the charge with a two-minute delay. Scottie would wave a red neckerchief as the gang approached so that there was no mistaking their arrival.

Wes's heart was beating fast and the palms of his hands were wet with sweat. He kept wiping them on his trousers, licking his lips and missing the odd swallow as his mouth dried up. What if it all went wrong? If Doyle got away from the set-up he'd shoot Alice for sure. It was too late now: everything was in place. Wes's eyes were fixed on the road away to the north of the town, waiting for a red flag signal.

The minutes passed. Wes could see a clock outside one of the town's gunsmiths. It was approaching one o'clock. He waited with baited breath but there was no sign of any red-flagged gang on the road. What could have happened? Jerry, the sheriff's full-time deputy, was posted in such a vantage point that he could keep an eye on Wes and make sure everything Wes had promised seemed to be in order. It had occurred to the sheriff that Wes's plan had in fact tied up all the deputies on the lookout for a raid that might not happen, maybe as a diversion.

Then, suddenly, there it was: the signal Wes had been waiting for. He lit the fuse; there was no going back. He waved to Jerry, who passed it on to the sheriff and so alerted the waiting posse stationed around the town. The bank was cleared and the employees, including the manager, scuttled across the street into the saloon opposite. Moments later all hell broke loose. The gang rode into Main Street, guns blazing into the air. Citizens dived this way and that, some under the boardwalk canopies, others dodging into alleyways or taking cover behind wagons and buggies. Folk on horseback scattered into back alleys, and the gang surrounded the bank entirely unopposed. Doyle and Davey went round the back to meet up with Wes. Berney and Kyle took up

118

positions by the front entrance. Scottie held the horses ready for getaway by an alleyway two streets behind the bank.

Restrained according to orders, all the new deputies, Jerry and the sheriff stayed under cover. Then the air was filled with a tremendous ear-splitting blast as a large section of the back wall of the bank crumbled into a pile of dust and debris, leaving the back of the safe exposed to daylight. Wes scrabbled over the rubble and placed a small charge with a very short fuse under the safe. The three of them took cover as a second explosion blew the metal back right off. At the front of the bank Berney and Kyle were watching Main Street nervously for signs of any lawmen. It didn't occur to them at first that the absence of any resistance from the town's citizens or lawmen was unusual, especially for a relatively large town like Courtney, or that the bank was empty of customers. Where were they hiding? Everyone had scattered from the street outside the bank, and the only movement came from the occasional dog and the suspended shop signs. But not everyone knew what was going on, and soon shots were being fired at Kyle and Berney by angry townsmen from a number of positions along Main Street.

Before they were properly ready for action, the sheriff took the initiative, fired the agreed signal and the deputies at the front of the bank ran out of cover toward the main door. Kyle and Berney fell back inside immediately and slammed the door shut. They smashed a window and returned fire.

At the back of the bank, Doyle, Davey and Wes had

119

filled saddlebags with bundles of cash and bonds. Hearing the firing in Main Street they took what they had and dodged through two alleyways to Scottie and the horses. Just as they emerged from the second narrow defile, a shot rang out and Wes fell back. Davey stopped and was about to help him.

'Leave him be!' Casey shouted as he leapt onto his horse.

Davey took a flying leap onto his mount immediately. There was no sign of Kyle or Berney, who should have been at the meeting place.

'Ride!' Doyle ordered. 'Ride! Go!'

Scottie took the lead and headed down his prepared route. Turning a sharp corner, not more than two blocks from the bank, they suddenly found their road barred by a line of men with rifles levelled. Pulling up sharply and turning in the dust, they were greeted by another group of riders closing in from behind. The sheriff's plan was perfect. If Scottie had not been so meticulous in his planning or had taken a different route from the one he and Wes had previously surveyed, they might have got away. There was nothing for it but to surrender. Doyle briefly thought that to go down fighting would be heroic, but a man who can slap, punch or inflict horrible pain on a woman is, at heart, a coward.

Once those three had been captured and were on their way to a secure lodging in the town's jail, Wes hurriedly retrieved his horse from the sheriff who, true to his word, let Wes escape on condition he never came to Courtney again. There was no news of Kyle or Berney, and Wes didn't wait to ask. He assumed they must have been slugged in the bank. There was no point in having any sympathy for any of the gang. Wes thought only of the men murdered in the raid on Gudrun's mine, of the bank clerk shot in Sweetspring and of the man left dead in the stagecoach. Those innocent people and their families were the ones who deserved his sympathy.

Weary with the effort of the day, but satisfied with the outcome, Wes finally arrived at the hollow. He fired two shots in quick succession, the usual friendly signal, but then realized that only Alice and Aimee would be at the camp. At least there would be a fire and food. On the lonely journey back to camp, and with mixed emotions about the betrayal and deception, Wes had been chewing over what to say to the two young women. At least there would be nobody to contradict his version of events. Even so, it required some thought as to how he was going to conclude his mission.

In a climate of extreme melancholy, the three of them sat together to eat. Wes began by recounting his version of the raid and why it all went wrong. The only difficult part was to explain how he fell before he could get on his horse and why the other three had ridden off without him. Luckily, as often happens when recounting events, the two listeners just accepted what was said as part of the narrative, made no comment and didn't dwell on any particular detail. Wes confirmed that Doyle, Davey and Scottie had been taken alive. He couldn't account for Kyle or Berney but believed them to be dead or they would have been at the meet to get their horses.

Keen to move on from what was essentially an untrue story, Wes turned to Aimee. He could see she had been crying quietly, knowing that gang leader Doyle was almost certain to hang for his crimes.

'What am I to do?' she sobbed rather feebly. 'Doyle is my life. There's no point in living without him.' Alice put her arm round Aimee to comfort her.

Wes sighed. For the first time he began to understand the full implication of what he was doing; the consequence of the ripples. There was no doubt in his mind that Doyle Casey and his gang had to be stopped. But he hadn't imagined scenes like this. He had no compunction about hunting down his old friend Doyle Casey, but he'd never expected to see Aimee Vangraf again in his life, or for such a meeting to rekindle long-forgotten feelings of tenderness. He wasn't a bounty hunter and he wasn't a killer: he was just doing what he believed was right, hoping to save his childhood friend from a life of crime and the inevitable hangman's noose. And, he had to admit, hoping to raise his own status in the eyes of Henry Mancini and win his consent to marry Maddy.

Sitting now in silence, as Aimee wept and Alice tried to comfort her, he saw things in a different light. What if it was Maddy sitting there weeping over him? Suppose the sheriff double-crossed him and a posse was already on its way to capture him in his bed, even to hang him as a dangerous robber? He would be torn to pieces for destroying Maddy's future happiness. Only the most hardened, drug-crazed, selfish ridge-riding loner can have no feelings for anyone but himself. Wes was overcome with compassion, his brain working overtime.

'Trust me, Aimee. Things will turn out all right, I promise. Everything can be put right.' But he had no idea yet as to how he could fulfil that pledge. Aimee continued to sob and Alice kept looking at him accusingly.

Wes pursed his lips. 'You have to trust me.'

Then Aimee, in her despair, delivered a devastating accusation. 'How do I know it wasn't your fault that everything went wrong with this raid? Doyle has been suspicious of you from the moment you arrived.'

'I know, I thought he was going to shoot me when he confronted me.'

'Maybe he should have, then he'd still be here.'

Wes made allowances for Aimee's grief and ignored the cutting remarks. Focused on trying to persuade Aimee that everything would work out, Wes hadn't noticed a figure creeping into the hollow.

Everyone was taken by surprise when a voice came out of the dark.

It was a squeaky voice, wobbling with incoherence and preceded by a stupid but familiar high-pitched little laugh. 'Yeah, maybe he should've shot you. Would've saved me the bother.'

Wes stayed sitting exactly where he was; one sudden or false move and this maniac would plug him.

'He's a smooth talker, ain't he, Aimee? Did he tell you how they were waiting for us, and how they rounded us up, all except me and Berney? Berney's dead: they shot him up good. I hid up in the bank. I could see the whole town gathered at the sheriff's office

123

to see Doyle, Davey and Scottie taken to the jail. But there wasn't no Wesley Vernon. *Where was Wesley?* I wondered. *Shot dead like Berney?'*

Kyle paused and laughed his irritating squeaky noise. He pulled something out of his mouth, bit a piece off and spat it out, then continued chewing on the wad, no doubt laced with resinous substances.

'Strange, ain't it, how he was the only one got away.'

Wes interrupted, 'I was lucky, that was all. So were you.'

'Sure you were. But your luck's run out now, you double-crossing sonofabitch.'

Kyle came forward into the light of the wood fire. His countenance was a horrible mixture of twisted glee and despicable satisfaction. He levelled his gun at Wes, held the revolver out at arm's length and squeezed the trigger. Wes was frozen to the spot. The hammer clicked, but there was no explosion of powder. Having failed to reload properly after the bank shootout, there were empty chambers in the cylinder. Kyle looked at his gun and levelled it again; it took no more than a split second. This time a shot filled the air with smoke, an ear-splitting noise, and a short licking tongue of fire.

Kyle was thrown back, stumbled and fell. He screamed in agony and squirmed on the ground. Wes leapt to his feet as a second shot rang out; Kyle's body humped with the impact and slumped motionless.

Alice stood up. She was shaking violently. Wes immediately grabbed her so she didn't fall over. He sat her down gently and took the gun out of her hand. Aimee was staring at her.

Alice's eyes were glazed over trance-like. 'I've never shot anyone before.'

Nobody knew what to say. Wes looked at the gun, a small silver-coloured four-shot large-calibre pistol, the one that Alice carried in her bag. He turned it around in his hand.

'It's a point four-one, whatever that means,' Alice added.

'It means it packs a helluva punch at short range. Enough to blow that no-good off his feet. Enough to save my life.'

'Colt made it. It's a new model. My father gave it to me as part of my travelling kit for the journey; said I'd be safer with it. He made me practice and wouldn't let me travel west until I could shoot a hole through a tin can on the wall.'

Wes walked over to Kyle's lifeless body. He eased the revolver out of his hand, released the cylinder slowly, noticed the empty chamber that had just been clicked and saw a bullet in the unfired chamber, the one that would have done for him.

Wes heaved a huge sigh. 'I don't like to be disrespectful of the dead but this man is the kind that makes life a misery for honest folk. He's better off out of it.'

Alice had regained her composure. 'Suppose I'd missed,' she said.

'Well, I, for one, wouldn't have known about it!' Wes proclaimed with a chuckle. 'Now, I suggest we get some sleep. We'll have to decamp early; this is no longer a safe place to stay.'

'What are we going to do?' Aimee wondered. 'Where

do we go?'

'You must go north to your ranch and wait there for me. I've promised you everything will turn out all right. Will you do that?'

'I guess I have no choice.'

'You don't. You must leave by sunrise. Alice and I will stay here another day for me to tie up some loose ends.'

Aimee accepted her instructions and with horrible feelings of loneliness and depression went off to spend a final night in the tarp and wood shack that had been her rough makeshift, but warm and cosy, home with Doyle. She thought of him in jail, lying on a hard wooden bed with maybe a blanket if he was lucky. She knew he would be thinking of her and fell asleep with that comforting thought.

Alice and Wes slept together under the same covers again, nothing more than like brother and sister, but Wes had his arms round Alice and he kissed her twice on the cheek, being so grateful for having the courage to take decisive action and saving his life. They both knew her first shot had been a lucky hit, just enough to buy a second of time. Wes knew it would take Alice a long time to get over her second bullet, which ended a man's life. Whether in self-defence or in defence of another innocent person, killing is still murder, however it is dressed up. Alice had crossed an invisible line, which even in the untamed west most people never went near, and certainly very few women. Crossing that psychological Rubicon lingers for a very long time.

Wes held her tight, remembering how he'd felt when

126

he killed for the first time, shooting to death Doug's partner, Donel. How life changes. How such things shape our future. How we never imagine the way our feelings can change. He pulled Alice closer, the warmth of her body, the round softness of her shape so comforting while he was lost in his own imaginings, knowing that the next day he would have to accomplish an action that was the most dangerous he had yet undertaken. His mind was a whirl of possibilities, assessing everything that might go wrong and probably would. But this situation was of his own making and now he had to see it through to the end.

13

Wes woke early. There was a faint light in the east and the sky was changing from coal black to Prussian blue. Stars shone but not so brightly. The air was sharp and cold. Mist hung over the pond. The fire was smouldering. Dressing hastily, Wes went over to the woodpile and selected some smaller logs with which to bring the embers back to life. He put some water in the iron kettle and settled it in the ashes to boil up for coffee. The fire crackled as the damp on the logs spat dry. He wondered whether he should wake Aimee already or let her sleep on. She would apparently have a long ride north to the ranch. At least he assumed Doyle hadn't lied about having a spread with cattle and horses. The water wasn't near boiling yet so he walked over to Aimee's shack and knocked lightly.

'Aimee,' he called softly, his mouth almost pressed onto the wooden door. There was no reply. 'Aimee,' he said, more distinctly. But still no answer. He eased the door open and looked in. It was too dark to see much, so he pushed the door wider and went in. The bed was empty. Aimee was gone.

He went back out quickly and checked the horses. One had gone. She must have left in the night. He hoped she had gone north as he told her; he hoped she would trust him to keep his word. Well, it was out of his hands now. He had to turn to his own plans. The water was boiling. He made some coffee, took out a smoke and settled himself on one of the old chairs by the fire. The problem he wrestled with was how to use the dynamite without killing anyone. That was the second problem; the first was how to get to the right place without anyone knowing.

He must have dozed off after the coffee, because he was suddenly aware of bright daylight. The sun was not yet over the mountaintop; that never happened in the hollow until almost midday, but it was obviously much later than he thought. Hastily he woke Alice and urged her to make him some breakfast while he made his preparations.

'Aimee has gone. She left in the night. It's just you and me now. I have some unfinished business to attend to tonight. I'll be back tomorrow morning and we'll pack up what we can and leave.'

'And go where?'

'You were going to Coldbush, I thought. We can go that way.'

'All right,' Alice replied without enthusiasm. Wes was too busy with his own thoughts to notice the tone.

His first job was to find some clothes that weren't his. He searched through the tents and the shack. He came up with enough, including a dark coloured slicker that he'd wear over everything else. He packed what he needed, which included two sticks of dynamite, put his saddle on one of the horses, and a spare saddle on another. He didn't want to use Ned in case he was recognized. He arranged a neckerchief such that it covered his lower face without making him look like a bandit and tied another round his forehead under his hat. He checked his Colt and Winchester, and slipped a knife into his boot. After breakfast he pulled Alice close for a brotherly kiss, but she moved her head and their lips brushed. Wes pulled back and said sorry, although it was Alice who had moved. He mounted quickly and set off down the mountain track.

Focused on keeping the horse off the slippery scree and steering it down the middle of the narrow defile, he licked his lips with concentration. Suddenly it dawned on him what Alice had done. She had tried to kiss him full on the mouth. It was unsettling. She was a companion in adversity; someone he had rescued and was taking care of, as any man would. Or maybe not. Perhaps other men would have tried to take advantage of her, pressed their unwanted attention on her. Wes's sense of honour, decency and his commitment to Maddy had subdued any male instinct towards Alice. But then, hadn't he also been cuddling her at night? Should he have refused to get under the covers with her when she wanted to be warmed up? Were his brotherly kisses being misunderstood and had he unwittingly been encouraging her?

Before he realized it, he was halfway to Courtney, having taken the road subconsciously without giving it any thought. Thoughts of Alice were set aside. His mind was now playing on the way he might acquire the information that he needed. He decided the best way would be to select a saloon in one of the back streets and listen for a chance to pump some barfly for news and gossip. Afraid to show his face in Courtney, he hung back from the town in a wooded area until dusk. He felt well disguised; a smear of charcoal from the fire that morning, carefully applied to his jowls, had increased his rather shabby, stubble-faced appearance. He certainly didn't look like the Wes Vernon that the sheriff or Deputy Jerry might remember.

Wes hadn't just stopped to lurk in the woods to pass the time of day. He was carefully assessing a location to leave the horses, so that he might make good his escape from the town on foot and still be able to find them in the dark. Having settled on a place, he hitched the horses, slipped the necessary equipment into the large inner pocket of the slicker and walked into town off the beaten track. He went into the first back street saloon that he found. It was dirty, noisy, and full of saddle tramps and assorted low life, women of easy virtue and waitresses who expected to have their rumps slapped when they delivered their drinks. An altogether unsavoury venue; exactly what Wes needed.

He ordered a beer from the barkeep and sat at a table with three other men who were arguing over some trifling matter.

'Good evening, gentlemen,' Wes began jovially. 'What'll you have to drink?'

It was the right kind of introduction in such a seedy

place, especially when you have not asked or been invited to sit at a table. The angry eyes of the three arguing men turned to grateful smiles at the offer of a drink. When the waitress came over with his beer Wes duly stroked her round rump and ordered three whiskeys. The waitress smiled as if the fondling was especially to her liking. Wes hid his displeasure and concentrated on wheedling some news. He set the ball rolling, knowing it would run of its own accord for a while.

'I heard the Casey gang has been caught. Luck run out at last.'

'Yeah, all shot to death.'

'No, no, Bart, that ain't right.'

'Yeah it is, me and Noddy were temporary deputies.'

'Nah, Bart, they're all in jail. Seen 'em myself. Three of 'em. Other three got shot.'

Wes added his bit. 'I heard one of them got away.'

'Mebbe. But I saw three in jail, so I know where they are.'

'All in the same cell?' Wes queried.

'You ain't seen 'em, Noddy.'

'Sure did,' Noddy confirmed. 'That Doyle Casey, proud as a peacock, all on his own. Reckon he demanded to have a cell all to hisself. Them other two squashed up in a little cell lying on their beds. Casey pacing about, telling the sheriff they'd never hang him.'

'How did you get to see 'em, Noddy?' Bart challenged, disbelievingly.

'Jerry's a friend of mine,' he replied haughtily. 'He

132

let me take a look.'

The conversation had gone far enough on the subject for Wes. He was anxious to change it in case it aroused any suspicion. He was after all a stranger in town asking about a notorious gang that had just been captured. In such a saloon, where anyone might be listening, someone was bound to notice that, and maybe report it to the sheriff.

Wes decided to make up an unlikely story. 'I heard they were surveying for a railway coming here from Bakersfield.'

'I heard exactly the same,' said Noddy, throwing the reliability of his information into serious doubt.

Undeterred, Wes spent the rest of the convivial evening in the company of these three local ne'er-do-wells. When it came time for the party to break up Wes managed to persuade Noddy to stay for another drink as the other two left.

'Were you telling the truth about seeing Casey in a cell on his own?'

Noddy was slightly the worse for the copious amount of whiskey that he had drunk. 'Sh . . . sh . . . sure, I seen 'im.'

'In a cell on his own? At the very back of the jail?' Wes knew he would have to ask direct questions and rely on a simple yes or no response from Noddy. A sentence of more than two words would be beyond his current capability.

'Yep.'

Wes pressed: he was only going to get one chance and the information had to be right. 'Right at the back, the last cell of them all? And was anyone in the cell next to him?'

'No.'

'Was there a small window, high up, with bars across?'

'Yessir.'

The interrogation could finish. Wes now knew exactly which cell Doyle was in. All he needed was a ladder. A short while later, Wes helped Noddy through the batwings; he was too unsteady on his own feet. But it wasn't for charity; Wes had an ulterior motive. He guided Noddy away from the saloon and through the back streets towards the back of the sheriff's office.

'Th'other way,' Noddy slurred.

'This way's quicker, you'll see. I know you live in the other direction but this is quicker.' Wes guessed that was what Noddy meant, but he had no fear that Noddy would either contradict him or make any fuss, since his brain was too fuddled. Reaching the back of the sheriff's office, Wes put his hand on the brickwork. It was not too solid. He looked up for the barred window and made Noddy stand underneath it. He pushed him back gently against the wall.

'Stand fast. Now hold your hands out.' He made Noddy cup his hands in his lap and told him he was going to put his foot there. 'Brace yourself, Noddy.'

In a swift but careful movement Wes stood first in Noddy's hands then up on his shoulders. He prayed that Noddy's legs would hold steady despite the amount of whiskey flowing in his veins. In case Noddy buckled, Wes gripped the iron bars of the cell window, little more than a slit in the brickwork. Not being able to get level with the window, which was too high, he spoke into the darkness and hoped for the best.

His voice was an urgent whisper. 'Doyle! Doyle! It's Wes.' There was no reply. He repeated himself. Then a response.

'Wes? What in hell?'

'Listen buddy, I'm going to blow a hole in the wall. Crouch in the corner and cover yourself with anything you've got, a blanket or anything. As soon as the hole appears, come out. Ready?'

'You bet!'

In less than three minutes the jail was shaken by a small explosion; a hole just about big enough for Doyle to crawl through had opened up. He left at once, met up with Wes and they were soon making their way through the back streets towards the woods and the horses. Before the fuse was lit, Noddy had been placed carefully in the alley beside the jail and left to sleep. He probably hadn't heard the bang. Nor would he hear the next three explosions, which went off at two-minute intervals all along the back street in the hope of delaying any search for Doyle while investigations were carried out.

Once the horses had been located, Wes told Doyle that Aimee had left for their ranch up north and that he should go there, too. Then he took hold of Doyle's arm.

'I'm not here to lecture you, old buddy, but for God's sake, give up this way of life and have a family with Aimee. I recognized you at the mine raid. When I set out from Sweetspring I wanted to bring you to justice. But I don't want to see you hang. I'd rather bring you to your senses. I'm doing this for Aimee as much as for you. Now get going.'

Doyle looked long and hard at Wes; all he could see was the whites of his eyes glistening with emotion. He hoped Wes couldn't see the same in his.

'I owe you,' Doyle said, then turned away quickly, leapt onto the horse and was gone.

Wes heaved a huge sigh of relief. Had he done the right thing? That man was a murderer, or at the very least he was responsible for killing and robbing. He had ruined the lives of too many honest men and women. But then Wes had always been taught that God welcomed sinners into his kingdom just as much as he welcomed honest folk. It was one of the mysteries of the world why that should be so. It seemed to mock honest folk if rogues, villains and murderers could also be let through those gates, even welcomed with open arms. Didn't the parable of the prodigal son teach us so? Even though Wes wasn't particularly assiduous about Bible study, everyone had heard about the prodigal son. And the West was full of them.

Wearily, Wes slipped away into the night, wishing that he had a few whiskeys to inflame his blood and warm his soul. With a bit of luck he could get some rest before he and Alice had to pack up and move out. Too many people knew the name of Two Trees Hollow, even if they didn't know exactly where it was and every bounty hunter in the neighbourhood would soon be hunting for Doyle Casey.

Wes fired the two shots to let Alice know that it was him. She was sitting by the fire, the kettle was boiling, bacon was sizzling on the griddle, the sun wasn't yet over the mountaintop and everything seemed good.

Rested and refreshed, Wes told Alice to gather anything she wanted; they wouldn't ever be coming back to the hollow again. This time she would have her own horse and there was another to act as pack animal. By mid-afternoon, they had cleared up as best they could. The place was to be left as tidy as they could make it. The beds were made up and the tents were tidied. It was a memorial site. Wes felt it was his duty to ensure Two Trees Hollow would never be used again. He sent Alice ahead down the track with the packhorse attached by a rope. He had dug the last two sticks of dynamite under the sheer face at the narrow entrance to the hollow. Now, on departure, he lit the long fuse and followed Alice down the track. When he was halfway down the mountain, the ground shook suddenly. A couple of dislodged boulders crashed down to the pines below. That shouldn't have happened, but up above, the entrance to the hollow had been completely blocked by the disintegration of the blown rock-face. Wes was satisfied with his handiwork, notwithstanding the two rogue boulders that had flown past him.

Ahead of them would be a night or two in the open.

'We're not going to Coldbush,' Wes said plainly. 'Too dangerous and too close to Courtney Crossing. We're going north on a circuit.'

Alice said nothing. Wes was thinking.

'You never did tell me why you were going to

137

Coldbush. Something to do with an uncle, was it?'

'He has a ranch and I'm going to live with him.'

'Suppose you tell me the truth for once,' Wes suggested.

'What do you mean?'

'You haven't got an uncle in Coldbush. No more than every girl has an uncle in Coldbush.' He paused. 'Or Courtney Crossing or Sweetspring.'

'What would you know about it?'

Wes laughed. 'I don't know anything about it, but you haven't asked me a single question about Coldbush or ranching or living out here in the west. You haven't mentioned your uncle, or cattle or anything. You haven't shown any curiosity whatsoever, and I find that a little puzzling.'

Alice said nothing. Wes was thinking.

'Did you have anything to do with that Emile Laroche from Boston?'

'I did not.'

'Or the dead man in the coach?' There was no answer to that question. 'He was going to California I seem to remember. A prospector, you said.' There was still no response. 'You see, I think you knew the dead man. You weren't travelling on your own, were you? All that about your father giving you the four-shot pocket Colt wasn't true, was it? You've been very quiet since the coach incident. What was that man to you? Tell me.'

'If I say anything, will you promise on your life that you won't leave me out here on my own?'

'Why would I do that?'

'You might not like what I'm going to say. But you

138

wanted the truth. Remember? He was my uncle.'

'Go on.'

'He was after gold, but not as a prospector. He was going to rob jewellery stores. He thought it would be easier with me posing as his wife and trying on rings and things, so he could slip some away without the storekeepers noticing. He was clever with his hands, could make a dollar coin disappear by rolling it over his fingers. Promised me we'd be rich in no time at all.'

'But he wasn't your uncle, was he?'

Alice looked away. 'No.'

'Were you in love with him?'

'No, never. He tricked me into coming west with him. I'm glad he's dead.'

That was enough for Wes; it had the ring of truth and he didn't want to press any further. It was probable the man had other ideas about making easy money with Alice. He didn't want to think about that. That night they slept together, Wes and Alice, still clothed but side-by-side under the stars, and for the first time, Wes wasn't thinking about Maddy.

14

Three days of skirting to the north brought them within striking distance of Sweetspring. Just one more night in the open and they would be back in habitation. Wes told Alice that she could stay with him for a day or two to find her feet, but then she would have to get her own accommodation as his intended girl, Maddy Mancini, the daughter of an important local businessman, who might eventually be running for state governor, would think it rather strange that he had come back home with a beautiful young woman in tow.

'You have aspirations for yourself and this girl? When her father is governor will you be an important person, too?'

'I don't know about that,' Wes said modestly. 'Her father doesn't actually like me, but we've been together, me and Maddy, for a long time. I did all this to impress her father.'

'This girl loves you?'

'I hope so.'

*

Morning came too soon, but Wes was up and scrounging for some dried wood to get the fire going for coffee and bacon. Alice rolled over and went back to sleep. Wes took pity and drank coffee on his own, ate all the bacon and sat smoking while Alice slumbered. In just these few days she had become an integral part of his life, almost as much of a reality as Maddy, maybe more so. In a strange way, having shared so much hazardous adventure, even in such a short space of time, made Wes feel almost closer to Alice than he did to Maddy, with whom he had shared very little besides the weekly dance. He pulled hard on his smoke and blew a thin line of bluish whiteness in a long straight line until it lost control of itself and disintegrated. It was a small reflection of how Wes felt about himself. The long straight line was in danger of disintegration.

Alice woke in due course. Wes cooked her a chunk of bacon and gave her a mug of coffee. He rather liked looking after this would-be jewellery thief, though he couldn't quite see her in that role. Alice was too smart for that kind of life. It even crossed his mind that she might have shot the man in the coach, the man who was forcing her into a life of crime and maybe worse. After all, she shot Kyle without hesitation. What would happen to her now? What sort of work could a woman on her own find that wasn't in some way disreputable? It bothered him a lot.

Not wanting to parade himself and Alice through the town, Wes brought them in from a northerly direction so he could get her to his shack without being noticed by more people than his immediate neighbours. The sun was on its way down. The sand was hot from the day. They approached Wes's shack and dismounted. He opened the gate and they went onto his patch of land. The horses were stabled and fed, saddles and harness were hung on the racks, all the equipment was offloaded and they went inside.

'This is a nice place,' Alice said, looking into the storeroom, the bedroom and all round the big living space with its range and big pine table complete with six chairs. 'Planning on having a big family?'

Wes ignored the question. 'You could get some wood in and light the fire in the range. It's in the shed by the stable.'

Alice went out. Wes threw some of his kit into the bedroom. He opened the window to air the room. A few moments later he was back in the living room wondering why Alice hadn't come back in with some wood. What was she doing? He went to the door to call out. As soon as he stepped onto the veranda, four men appeared with rifles levelled. One of them was holding Alice by the arm. Shocked and confused, Wes immediately put his hands in the air. He recognized no one.

'Hold on!' he said. 'I ain't done nothing.'

Sheriff Sam Cottrell stepped out of the shadows. 'I'm sorry to be doing this, Wes, but I've a warrant to arrest you for the hold-up and robbery of a stagecoach near Coldbush.'

'You're joking, of course.'

Sam Cottrell shook his head. 'I wish I was, son.'

'But it isn't true, ask Alice, she'll tell you. Alice!'

'All in due course, son. Now, are you coming quietly?'

As he was led away, he said to Alice, 'Stay in my house while this is cleared up. I'll be back soon.'

Wes sat disconsolately on the hard bed in the cell. Was this how Doyle had felt that night, double-crossed somehow and trapped, without hope of someone stepping up to put in a good word? And who'd blow a hole in the wall for Wes? No, surely this was some mistake. There'd be a rational explanation. He couldn't blame Sam Cottrell for doing what he had to do. The real question was the source of the lies that had given rise to the warrant. Maybe Maddy would come and see him. Would her father put in a good word? Unlikely.

A waitress from the Grand Hotel brought a plate of dinner over for Wes. The sheriff brought it to the cell.

'Sam, what's going on? This hold-up. You know that's not like me.'

The sheriff passed the plate under the cage door. 'I guess I was mighty surprised. But when the information was laid I called the town council to get their views. They were astonished, but then they remembered that you were at the raid on the mine, you were in Main Street when they shot up the hotel. You were by the bank when that was attacked and Charlie Dobson was shot. Did you know Doc Willan couldn't save him? And when the posse found you, you had a superficial injury. We stopped the chase to look after you and the gang got away. Then a couple days later you buy new guns from Hagen's gun store and disappear. None of that

143

looks good, does it?'

'But I went after the gang. I caught up with them. Two are dead and two are in jail. That's my doing. And I believe someone on the town council may be in on those raids; that's why I didn't say anything at the meeting you invited me to attend.'

The sheriff sucked in some air. 'That's all pretty thin, Wes. Where's your proof?'

'I heard all this from two fellas, Doug and Donel, two . . .' he was about to say *ridge riders*, but realized it wouldn't help. And if enquiries were made at Courtney Crossing, his part in the escape of Doyle Casey might become known, and helping a murderer to escape would certainly merit a death sentence. He took the plate of food and thanked the sheriff. Something would turn up. He hoped so.

The sheriff was just leaving the cells. He offered what he thought was a crumb of comfort. 'I've already sent someone to make enquiries at Coldbush. Don't worry Wes. If you're innocent, you'll be out in a couple days.'

It wasn't what Wes wanted to hear.

The following morning, Wes was given some breakfast. Sam Cottrell had a soft heart underneath his craggy exterior and had some bacon and eggs sent over from the hotel. Few prisoners got anything from the sheriff except water and an occasional coffee if they kept quiet.

'I appreciate this, Sam,' Wes said taking the plate.

'I'll make some coffee in a minute. I've got someone coming in to see you later.'

'Maddy?' Wes hoped with excitement in his voice,

knowing that she would speak to her father who carried the most weight on the town council and could be persuaded to speak up for him.

The sheriff made no reply to that but went back into his office to make some coffee.

An hour passed, maybe two, before Wes heard people entering the sheriff's office and the sound of conversation. The door to the cells opened and the sheriff came through. Behind him, Wes couldn't at first see who the two visitors were, a man and a woman.

Sam brought them down to the cell. Wes was flabbergasted; this was the last person he expected to see.

'Are you sure this is the man who held up the stage?' the sheriff asked.

'Yes, I'm sure. This is Wesley Vernon: murderer, robber and torturer. Ask him about Two Trees Hollow.'

Wes looked from the man to the young woman in complete disbelief. Was this really happening? Why didn't she say something? As they turned to go, Wes found his voice.

'Maddy! What is this?'

The man rounded on Wesley. 'Don't address my wife in that familiar tone.'

'What?'

Maddy looked down and mumbled. 'I'm sorry, Wesley. Emile and I were married a few days ago.'

The sheriff ushered them out of the cell wing and closed the door. Gripping the bars tightly, Wes was left in a state of total shock. The sonofabitch Laroche hadn't taken his advice and gone east; he'd carried on his journey to do business with Mancini and claim his bride. Oh, how he wished he'd finished him off when he had the chance. How could Maddy be so fickle; it was all down to her father, he never wanted Maddy to marry Wes. It seemed nothing that Wes could have done would ever have changed his mind. All this effort in chasing Casey's gang had been a waste of time, even worse. If he'd kept out of it, Casey would eventually have killed Laroche; it was obvious he would do so. Wes had saved him to be repaid like this.

Disbelief now turned to outrage and anger. He smashed his fist into the cell wall. What could be done? Who was going to speak up for him? There was only one person could now do that.

'Sheriff! Sheriff! Sam Cottrell!' Wes called out, rattling the cell door. The sheriff opened the door to his office. 'Alice. Get Alice, she'll tell you different.'

'Calm down, Wes. The circuit judge is due in a couple weeks. I've got a lot of work to do to get all the evidence together. It's my job to bring you to trial. I ain't taking sides, just doing what I have to. You'll be wanting a lawyer, I guess.'

'No. I'm innocent. I don't need a lawyer to explain that.'

'A lawyer will put your case without getting emotional. The charges are serious.'

'I don't have to be told that. Please get Alice and talk to her.'

Wes was confident that as soon as Alice was told he was going to be held in the cell until the circuit judge arrived, she'd be in to see him straight away. Together they'd think of something. Alice was his best hope.

'She has already been in, you know. She asked me exactly what charges and I told her. The stagecoach hold-up, the murder of a male passenger, the detention and torture of Mr Laroche of Boston, the killing of the driver and shotgun rider and the theft of property.'

'She didn't ask to see me?'

'No.' The sheriff stroked his moustache. 'Matter of fact, she left in rather a hurry. I'll send someone out to tell her you want to see her.'

Wes began to run over all the evidence that Laroche might put before the judge. Laroche knew too much about the gang, about the Two Trees camp and could present a compelling case from the witness stand. If Sam had sent someone out to Coldbush asking questions, then that would inevitably lead to Courtney Crossing and the sheriff there would provide a lot of circumstantial evidence. The link with explosives, the bank and the jailbreak would be difficult to dispute. The sheriff of Courtney would see it all in a different light.

At last Wes heard people entering the sheriff's office. At least he'd have the comfort of seeing Alice and talking to her.

Sam Cottrell came into the cells, he looked rather gloomy. 'It's not good news, Wes. I'm sorry to have to tell you Alice is nowhere to be seen. There is no sign of her and one of the horses in your stable has gone.'

Wes sank down onto his hard wooden bed, his head in his hands. He couldn't grasp the situation. 'What about Ned? Someone's got to look after him while I'm stuck in here.'

147

'Tor Gudrun has already come forward to help you. He's the only one spoke up for you at the town council meeting. I'll talk to him about Ned; don't worry. Tor will arrange someone to feed and exercise him.'

'Thanks,' Wes said feebly. He'd even like to see Ned and talk to him. The world was a very black place and the only comfort Wes could imagine was that the blackest hour is the one before dawn.

'I expect Tor will come in and see you.'

Better than a crumb of comfort: that was a hunk of bread. Maybe Tor would have some ideas. Wes asked Sam if he could have some paper and a pen. He decided that to write everything down as he remembered the events of the last dozen extraordinary days would help him present a case when he was confronted by the circuit judge and the jury. Sam came back to the cell with a wad of paper, some of it old wanted posters which he said Wes could write on the back of. He gave him a pen and a small jar of ink.

'In your position I think I would start to write a confession,' Sam advised. 'I know the judge, and he is always lenient on people who own up to what they've done.'

'But I haven't done anything wrong.'

'That fellow suggested I should ask you about Two Trees. What was that?'

'Casey's hideout on High Top range. I sealed it off when me and Alice left, so nobody could get in there and use it again.'

'Or so nobody could get in there to look for any evidence.'

148

Wes was deflated. Everything he said could be turned round against him. He shrugged, took the paper, pen and ink and using his wooden bed as a table began to set down his recollections.

Life behind bars got more difficult. Some people say you get used to things in time, but Wes was straining at the leash. He felt like a hobbled horse longing to run wild and free. The confinement was beginning to affect his mental state. He'd seen caged animals pace up and down, just moving about pointlessly, now he realized they did it to get rid of pent-up energy. Any movement was better than inertia. The days passed and he slept more and more; an intolerable lethargy was creeping into his bones and his brain.

Desperate for conversation, he asked Sam to see if Maddy would come and explain what had happened, how she had got married to Laroche so quickly, but her father wouldn't allow it. Tor Gudrun visited Wes, as did some of his friends at the mine, but nothing could shift him out of the quicksand which would soon swallow him up. He kept asking Sam if any evidence had been found, but Sam remained tight-lipped, and nothing was said about Coldbush or Courtney Crossing. Eventually the days and nights merged into unremitting boredom. Then the circuit judge arrived.

Sam told Wes that his case would probably last two days, there being such serious charges against him. He checked whether Wes was still determined to defend himself rather than let a lawyer do it. Tor Gudrun had offered to act for him, but Wes was convinced that no jury of honest men from Sweetspring would find him guilty.

Having spent the first day listening to civil cases, adjudicating on land disputes, neighbour complaints, licensing infringements and other minor affairs, the judge retired to his suite in the Grand Hotel for the night. After he had dined, he walked across to the sheriff's office and was shown into the cells. Wes jumped to his feet when the sheriff introduced Judge Buckley. He stood in front of Wes, looking him over and scrutinizing his face. It was unsettling.

The judge cleared his throat. 'I can usually tell if a man is guilty before he even gets into court. I can see it in his eyes. The fear of the rope, the fear of dying, the recollection of the foul deeds he has committed and his hopeless pleas for mercy. There is no mercy in this life for people who commit the heinous crimes with which you are accused, young man. Society demands that you pay for the lives that you've taken.'

'But . . .'

The judge raised his hand. 'You'll have your chance to speak tomorrow from the witness stand. I understand you don't want a lawyer. Foolish decision: lawyers argue a case so much better than the accused. I see a fear in your eyes, sonny. You'd best pray hard tonight.'

Wes licked his lips. His mouth was as dry as the desert. He watched the judge and the sheriff leave the cellblock. The door closed. Wes was a wreck; his heart was beating fast. He felt that he hadn't a true friend in the world, anyone he cared for had deserted him and nobody but Tor had come forward to offer any encouragement. But then if they thought he really had committed all those things, he couldn't really blame anyone for passing him by.

Sleep that night was fitful, intermittent and punctuated by horrible dreams. He was glad when morning came and Sam Cottrell arrived with some coffee and breakfast. Then the time dragged until Sam returned mid-morning with two deputies and iron shackles. Chained like a wild animal and hobbled with the leg irons, Wes was taken the short distance from the cell to the courthouse, which was packed with the good citizens of Sweetspring. The judge's assistant rapped on the desk and the conversation melted into an eerie silence. Wes was taken to the prisoner's chair and the two deputies stood either side.

The assistant rapped the desk again. 'All rise. His honour Judge Desmond Buckley presiding.'

The judge came in to the courthouse and sat in the high chair. He put a wad of papers in front of him, moved a few things round on the desk, poured himself a glass of water, and nodded to the assistant. The assistant asked Wes to confirm his name, then read out the extensive list of charges. At the end Wes was asked to plead.

'Not guilty,' he said, but the words stuck in his throat. He coughed and tried again. 'Not guilty.'

15

Sam Cottrell did his best to read out the several pages of evidence that he had gathered together, mostly from the witness statement of Mr Emile Laroche, respected banker from Boston in the state of Massachusetts. The scene that was painted was backed up with the names, dates and times of all the various offences. Wes looked hard at Laroche during all the time that the evidence was being read out, but Laroche never once looked at Wes. From time to time, Laroche's wife, Maddy, Wesley's one-time sweetheart, shot a nervous glance in his direction, well-disguised by her handkerchief or some such subterfuge so that her husband wouldn't notice. Those glances cut Wes to the quick far more painfully than any of the lies that were being aired in the court.

After bits of clarification from the judge, Wes was at last given his turn to cross-examine Laroche. He maintained a steady voice, and for the first time his direct gaze met with Laroche's shifty eyes.

'Do you remember the night I cut you free? The

night I took your leg shackles off, cut the rope from your wrist and told you to go back east to avoid capture? Do you remember what I did for you that night?'

Laroche cleared his throat and spoke directly to the judge. 'I remember the night very well. It was exactly as he says. He cut the rope and freed the shackles, and told me it would be dangerous to go anywhere except back east, or I would be captured and probably killed.'

'He helped you to escape?' the judge asked, confused.

'Yes.'

The judged pressed further. 'Why did he do that?'

Wes was too inexperienced to challenge that question. A lawyer most certainly would have demanded that it be withdrawn since the witness could have no idea what was in the mind of the accused at the time.

'I think he knew that if he was caught I would be able to provide enough evidence about the hold-up to have him arrested and convicted of murder and robbery.'

'Which is exactly the case, is it not?' the judge pointed out.

'It is, your honour,' Laroche confirmed with satisfaction.

Wes intervened. 'You're saying that I let you go to save my own skin rather than as an act of mercy to save your life? You know very well they took you as a hostage and would've killed you eventually.'

The judge leapt on that. 'You don't know that for sure, do you? That he would have been killed.'

'I know it as surely as I know that my action was designed to save his life.'

'But,' said the judge, 'we only have your word on that. The word of a man accused of the most base actions and crimes against the word of a respected banker who has, despite the danger that you spoke of, nevertheless travelled on, not east but west, in order to fulfil contracts with Mr Mancini, a leading citizen of Sweetspring. It would appear that Mr Laroche is a man of his word, irrespective of any personal danger. I don't suppose the gentlemen of the jury will find it difficult which of you to believe.'

The judge looked to the jury. 'Consider this first session carefully; I think we have nearly learnt all we need to know. We've no need to waste time. We can conclude this afternoon.' He raised his hammer and hit the desk. 'The court will recess for lunch and reconvene at two o'clock sharp.'

Wes was taken back to his cell, given a plate of beans and left to think things over. If he'd been given a knife with his food he'd have considered cutting his throat. He pushed the beans round the plate. The judge had already made up his mind, that much was clear. If he steered the jury in the direction of a guilty verdict, Wes's fate was sealed. It would be an ignominious end to a heroic endeavour.

At five minutes to two, Wes was taken back into the courthouse. All stood while Judge Buckley came in and sat down. Wes looked at him closely. For the judge, this was just another trial, another day in court. It would end with a fine dinner in the hotel and a good night's sleep in a comfortable bed. Wes couldn't have felt more dejected. The afternoon's evidence began with one of

154

Cottrell's deputies taking the oath before reporting on his trip to Coldbush. Things were about to get a whole lot worse. Wes slumped in his chair. But nobody had noticed a masked man enter the court, behind the judge's dais. Not until he fired a shot into the roof. The courthouse went suddenly silent.

'Sit still, everybody!' the gunman said, approaching the judge's chair. Then with one gun still pointing at the roof and a second close to the judge's head, he stood tall and continued.

'You are blind fools. In the accused's chair is one of the most honourable and upright men I have ever had the privilege to know. In the witness stand is a man of very doubtful integrity, a banker from way back east. Why is he here? Probably to conduct illicit business with some important person in the town. I don't know, but I doubt that anybody will gain from the deal except himself and whoever he's doing business with.'

The gunman paused to raise the sense of tension. From the corner of his eye he saw a man trying to ease his way towards the door. He fired one shot into the wall in his direction and the man scuttled back to his seat.

'The next shot will be for the judge.'

The judge stiffened, visibly shaken. 'Listen, whoever you are, what is your evidence? Have you got something to prove who you are or the truth of what you're saying?'

'I have,' he took the mask off. 'I'm Doyle Casey. This man, Wesley Vernon, tracked down my gang single-handed. Yes, we've committed robbery, murder, hold-ups and more. I'm responsible for that stage hold-up. We carried out the raid on Gudrun's mine and the other things here in Sweetspring.'

Casey threw down a big bundle of cash onto the desk.

'This covers everything we stole from Sweetspring. I'm sorry about the lives that were lost, but nothing can be done about that. So, why am I here? A young lady rode north to find me and tell me what you fools were doing. You'd have hanged an innocent hero, a man of the highest integrity, simply because you think a banker's word is worth more. Well, it ain't. An' I'll tell you another thing. This man could have killed me a number of times. Could have left me to face the ultimate penalty for murder. But instead of that he made me see that my life of crime was useless. He gave me another chance. I owe it to him to see that he doesn't pay the penalty for your stupid prejudices.'

He turned to the judge. 'Direct the jury now to acquit this man and record it in the court papers.' He cocked his revolver close to the judge's ear. It was unnecessary but impressive.

'Case dismissed,' the judge said with resignation. He picked up the pen and entered the verdict into the court record.

Casey turned to the accused. 'Good luck, Wes. There's a good woman waiting in Coldbush to start a new life with you. I've given her the deeds to my ranch. Marry her and it's yours. Aimee and I are taking the herd and going north, a long way north to raise the beef and maybe a family.'

Then, just as suddenly as he had entered, Doyle

Casey slipped out the back, both guns blazing and a barrage of shots crashing into the ceiling. Bits of plaster fell onto the stunned crowd, their ears bursting with the noise as the room filled with acrid smoke. For a moment, everything was in slow motion, and then people began to run for the exit in an undignified and unnecessary panic. They spilled out into Main Street, bewildered. Sam Cottrell and a deputy had hold of Mr Emile Laroche, banker of Boston, Massachusetts.

Henry Mancini went over to them. 'I'll look after Emile, Sam. No need for any fuss.' He led Laroche away.

Outside the courthouse, Tor Gudrun shook Wes by the hand. 'I suppose I'll be looking for a new explosives foreman.'

'Guess you will, and thanks for standing by me. How's Ned? Fit and well, I hope. I shall clear out tomorrow; there's nothing for me here except disappointment and bad memories.'

'And there's someone waiting for you at Coldbush.'

'Yes, it seems so. Give my shack to your new mine engineer. I don't need it any more, and thanks for looking after Ned. You know, Tor, I'll just say this. I suspected someone on the town council was passing information to Casey's gang and . . .'

'Forget it, Wes. There's always corruption where money is concerned. If anyone's doing anything wrong it'll come to light one day. You just get on with building a new life. Tell me, is the young lady pretty?'

'Pretty? There's more to it than that! She's someone with determination, a warm heart and courage beyond

157

the ordinary.'

'That's good, then.'

Wes laughed. 'And she's damn pretty too!'

That night Wes spent some minutes talking to Ned, grooming him ready for the journey back to Coldbush. He put together the few things that he couldn't live without and settled down for the last night in his Sweetspring shack. Early the next morning, before sunrise, he loaded his goods onto Ned, mounted and set off for a new life. It wasn't so many days ago he'd done exactly the same thing, not knowing what he would find. Nor so many days since he had first set eyes on a young lady who tried to steal his horse. She didn't succeed in that, but over the following days she had succeeded in stealing something equally precious: his heart. In a couple days' time they would be back together and riding north to Casey's ranch. Ironic really, Wes thought to himself. Alice had said all along that she was going to live with her uncle on his ranch. Wes hadn't really believed her, and he certainly wasn't her uncle, but in a strange turn of events, it seemed her fabricated story might come true.

Wes wondered if Doyle would leave him any beef to start off a new herd. Both he and Alice had a lot to learn, but he had never felt so excited. The miles to Coldbush couldn't pass quickly enough. It was a two-day ride, and it was late afternoon on the second day when Wes hitched outside Nooner's saloon. He pushed through the batwings and went up to the counter.

'Nooner! A large beer, if you please!' he demanded.

But a voice said, 'There's already one here waiting.'

Wes swung round and saw Alice. There was a glass of beer on the table. She smiled and patted the empty chair.

Nooner whistled through his lips and shook his head. 'About time, sonny. She's been waiting there all day.'